g lyrics in Ch. 7 adapted from William
espeare's *As You Like It*.

a work of fiction. References to historical
organizations, events, places, and
ments are the product of the author's
n or are used fictitiously.

Clockpunk Press

2956-0367
press.com
957517
X
n Amick
esign by Damonza.com
Interior Book Designing

CHASING

the

GREEN FAIRY

ALSO BY MELANIE KARSAK

The Harvesting Series:
The Harvesting

The Airship Racing Chronicles:
Chasing the Star Garden (Book I)
Forthcoming: Chasing the Fog (Book III)

Also Forthcoming:
Lady Macbeth; Wyrd Queen of Scotland

CHASING

the

GREEN FAIR

MEI

Published by
PO Box 56036
Rockledge, FL
www.clockpunk
ISBN-13: 978-0615
ISBN-10: 061595751
Edited by Cat Carlso
Cover art and book d
Formatting by Inkstai

Sor
Sha

This is
people,
establishi
imaginatio

CLC

THE AIRSHIP RACING CHRONICLES II

CHASING

the

GREEN FAIRY

A sabotaged airship.

A recovering opium addict.

A messenger with life-shattering news.

With the 1824 British airship qualifying race only weeks away, Lily Stargazer is at the top of her game. She's racing like a pro, truly in love, and living clean. But on one ill-omened day, everything changes.

Pulled head-long into the ancient secrets of the realm, Lily soon finds herself embroiled in Celtic mysteries and fairy lore. And she's not quite sure how she got there, or even if she wants to be involved. But Lily soon finds herself chasing the spirit of the realm while putting her own ghosts to rest. And only accepting the truth—about her heart and her country —can save her.

In memory of Barbara

CHAPTER 1

A CHARTREUSE-COLORED LEAF FLUTTERED DOWN onto the wheel of the *Stargazer*. It was early morning. The mist covering the surface of the Thames reflected the rosy sunrise. Yawning, I reached out to brush it away only find it was not a leaf at all. Carefully, I balanced the fragile creature on the tip of my finger.

"Mornin', Lil. Hey, what's that?" Jessup called as he bounced onto the deck of the *Stargazer*.

Angus was cursing as he cranked out the repair platform below the ship. We were preparing for our morning practice run to Edinburgh.

"A luna moth," I replied.

"I thought maybe you'd finally caught the green fairy," Jessup joked as he climbed into the burner basket.

I grinned. The moth's green wings, dotted with yellowish eyes, wagged slowly up and down. It was beautiful, but it was dying. "My mother once told me that they are fey things, that they live in the other realm until it's their time to die. Then, they come to humans."

"Why?" Jessup asked as he adjusted the valves. Orange flame sparked to life.

"She said that even enchanted things want to be truly loved at least once."

"Don't we all?" he replied with a laugh.

A harsh wind blew across the Thames, clearing the morning mist. It snatched the delicate creature from my hands. I tried to catch it, but the breeze pulled it from me even as it was dying. I lost it to the wind.

I sighed heavily as I picked up my tools then bounded over the side of the ship to the repair platform. I pulled out a dolly and rolled under, joining Angus who had fallen remarkably silent. The moment I saw the gear assembly on the *Stargazer*, I understood why.

"What the hell?" I whispered.

"Aye, lassie."

"Jessup!" I shouted. "Get the tower guards down here!"

"What's wrong?" Jessup called.

"The *Stargazer* has been sabotaged!"

I stared at the mangled gears. From the saw marks on the gear assembly to the metal shrapnel blown around the galley, it was clear what had happened. I felt like someone had punched me in the gut.

Seconds later I heard Jessup's boots hit the platform and the sound of him running toward the guard station.

"They removed Sal's torque mechanism. Sawed the bloody thing right off," Angus said angrily.

"But . . . who?" I stammered.

"The Dilettanti?" Angus offered as he strained to examine the rest of the assembly.

"No," I said as I touched the saw marks. The rough metal cut my finger. "That business is finished. Byron saw to that." I stuck my bloodied finger in my mouth. The salty taste of blood mixed with the tang of gear grease.

"Then who?"

"Someone who didn't want us to race in the qualifying. Someone who wanted to learn what had us running so fast."

We were less than a month out from the British qualifying. While there were other good race teams in the realm, no one raced better than us. After all, we were the champions of the 1823 World Grand Prix. My stunt in Paris had brought us heaps of acclaim, but not all our British competitors were impressed. Envy had set in.

"Grant?" Angus suggested.

Julius Grant, whose team was sponsored by Westminster Gas Light, was our greatest competition at home. He hated us. He was annoyed that we were sponsored by Byron, annoyed that I was female, and annoyed that we were faster than him. Grant was the most likely suspect. But he was not the only one. "Almost too obvious. What about Lord D?" I wondered aloud.

"He'd love to, but he doesn't have the stones," Angus replied. "Might be someone who doesn't want us in the Prix. If they take us out during qualifying, we aren't a threat abroad."

"That means it could be anyone."

"Hell, maybe one of Byron's lovers took a stab at you."

"But I'm not even romantically involved with him anymore."

"The rest of the world doesn't know that."

I rolled out from under the ship. Leaning against the *Stargazer*, I wiped my hands. The cut stung as grease mingled with the open wound. I wanted to either beat someone to death or cry. I wasn't sure which. Maybe both.

Angus joined me.

"Can we get it fixed in time?" I asked him.

He wiped sweat from his bald head as he thought. "It'll be close. I'll need Sal's help."

"You? Need Sal?"

"Aye, lassie."

"He's busy getting the factory ready, but he'll come."

Jessup returned with Edwin, the stationmaster, and Reggie, one of the guards.

"Where the hell were your people last night?" Angus demanded of Edwin. We'd known Edwin for a long time, and we trusted the guards in London. Something wasn't right.

As Angus and Edwin discussed, a terrible ache rocked my stomach. I set my hand on the side of the *Stargazer*. Her honey-colored timbers shone in the sunlight. Just as sleek and beautiful as she was the first time I laid eyes on her, she was my pride and joy. My ship. My love. I closed my eyes and took a deep breath.

"What do you think, Lil?" Jessup asked.

Clearly, I'd missed something. "Pardon?"

"Edwin suggested we post a private guard," Jessup explained.

I nodded. "We'll sort it out."

"Lily, I'm so sorry. Someone must have sneaked past us. I can't believe it," Edwin said. His clear blue eyes were brimming with tears.

I set my hand on his shoulder. "Who was stationed on this end last night?"

"Morton."

I sighed. I wasn't one to point fingers, but that explained it. "Was he still drunk when he went home this morning?" I asked Reggie.

Reggie shifted uncomfortably as Edwin turned to look at him. "He was," Reggie answered after a moment.

"That lazy, rummy bloke. I'll kill him! I'll kill him!" Edwin shouted, and in an angry huff, stomped back down the platform.

"Sorry, Lily. Angus. Jessup. I won't take my eyes off her," Reggie said sadly then went to take a post near the *Stargazer*.

"We'll sleep on the ship until we get a guard on board," I told Angus and Jessup who nodded in agreement.

"A guard . . . but who can we trust?" Jessup asked.

"The *Stargazer* is family. We need family to keep her safe," Angus replied then looked at me.

"You mean . . . Duncan?" About three years earlier, I'd been, albeit briefly, in a relationship with Angus' older brother Duncan. While I'd fallen for Duncan the moment I'd laid eyes on him, we were not suited for one another. Back then, I wasn't ready to give up Byron or anything else.

Angus shrugged. "I suppose he's over you by now."

"That's all well and good," Jessup spat, "but we need someone to look into this! Someone needs to be held accountable! We should send for the Bow Street boys."

Angus shook his head. "Only if we want everyone in London to know."

"Well, we need to do something!" Jessup protested.

"Let's keep it quiet. I'll talk to Phineas," I replied.

Jessup nodded eagerly. "Yeah. Good idea."

Angus frowned. "Are you sure about that?"

Phineas and I had a convoluted opiate history, but as Angus knew well, I'd been keeping my habits in check. "It'll be fine. I'll check in with Phin, go get Sal, and come back. We can head out to the league meeting together."

"If Grant looks even a wee bit guilty, I'm going to squeeze his neck," Angus cursed.

"If he looks guilty, I'll help you," I replied. I set my hand on the *Stargazer*. It was so painful to see something you loved damaged.

"It'll be all right, Lil," Jessup said trying to comfort me. "We'll get her fixed."

I smiled weakly at Jessup then turned to leave. I knew he was right, but it didn't make me feel any better.

CHAPTER 2

I RAPPED ON THE DOOR of Phineas' home, a well-appointed townhouse situated just off Hyde Park, clacking the brass bumblebee door clacker loudly. I waited for what felt like an eternity. On both sides of Phin's townhouse, the neighboring residences had arched foyers. The vista gave me vertigo. I was about to bang again when the butler, but not Phin's usual man, opened the door.

"Yes?" the man asked, looking me over from head to toe.

"Yes? I'm here to see Phineas."

"Master Shaw is not in."

"Yeah, that's a lie. Tell him Lily is here."

The man frowned then closed the door. I sighed and waited. The butler returned several minutes later.

"My apologies, Miss Stargazer. Mr. Shaw had indicated he was not permitting guests, but he said I may let you in. He is in the conservatory," the butler said. "You may see yourself back."

"What's your name?"

"Kent."

"Kent. Nice to meet you. In the future . . . well, Phin always sees me."

"So he indicated. I do wish he'd said so before," the man said with an exasperated expression. "Pleased to meet you, Miss Stargazer."

"Call me Lily," I said with a smile then headed toward the back.

Phineas' house was a hodgepodge of the odd and unusual. You could barely blaze a path through the ornate sculptures, carved masks, tinkered contraptions, tables crowded with jars of god-only-knew-what, and a copious amount of plants. Now and then, you even had to duck a bird flitting past. I stopped to look at a locked box with a human skull on its lid. Shaking my head, I wound my way back. The glass-roofed conservatory, situated at the center of Phin's odd little house, allowed him to grow his herbals in private. And there, amongst all the wildly growing plants, I found Phineas, shirtless, pouring a bubbling yellow liquid into a copper pot.

"Have a seat, Lily. Almost done," he said.

I looked around. There were no chairs anywhere, but I spotted a large tribal drum. I sat on it and watched him work.

"What's brewing?" I asked as I eyed Phineas over. He looked paler than usual. His face looked drawn, and though it was rather cool, he was sweating profusely. His auburn-colored hair, wet with sweat, stuck to his head, and he'd grown a moustache since the last time I saw him.

"I think I've finally got a good extraction of refined opium," he said. "A tinker at the market made me a device to spin the tinctures, to separate them at a higher velocity than ever before. I'm getting much more refined products now."

Phineas and I had once shared a passion for opium. For me, it had been a passion of habit, a way to dull the pain. For him, it was a passion of science. Phineas had an eye for detail, understanding a puzzle down to its very roots. While nothing escaped him, he put much of his mental energy toward herbals. Sometimes he was after medicine. Sometimes he was after pleasure. As I watched him work, I tried not to think about smoking opium. But it was impossible. Around me, beds of opium flowers were in full bloom. Heaps of the dried herbs littered a nearby table. I was ashamed of the craving it caused.

"There," he said, stirring the pot. "We'll know in an hour. Too bad you aren't in the habit anymore. We could try it together."

"You look like you could use a break. And a nap. And a meal."

Phineas shrugged. He mopped off his forehead and wiped down his armpits and chest. His skin was pasty, and he looked like he'd lost weight. His pants were hanging low on his waist. I tried not to notice the dark hair trailing down from his bellybutton below his belt. I looked away as he pulled on his shirt. I wondered if I used to look like him, a bit eaten up, when I'd let my habit get the best of me. "Tea?" he asked.

"Sure."

Phin motioned for me to follow him to his small kitchen at the back of the house. After clanging around in the cupboards for several minutes, he retrieved a teapot. It took him two tries, but he finally filled it with water and set it to heat. "So . . . what brings you by?" he asked, flopping into a chair across from me.

"Someone tampered with the *Stargazer*."

"Tampered?"

"Removed one of our modified devices. Sabotaged the ship."

Phineas got up and looked in his cupboards again. "I don't have any sugar."

"That's fine."

Phin's hands shook as he prepared the tea. The china clattered.

"Sit down," I said then got up and started preparing the cups.

"A woman's hand is sweeter anyway," Phineas said then sat again. "The *Stargazer*... that's awful," he said, picking a tobacco pipe up off the table. "I'll come by tomorrow and have a look, start talking to people. Surely someone saw something. I'll get to work."

"Don't forget," I warned. Phineas *was* great at sorting out details when he was himself. Right now, however, he was seeing the stars.

"Forget what?" he joked.

I grinned and shook my head. I went back into his cupboards for another look around. Inside, I found a jar of jam. There was a box of biscuits on the counter. I spread the jam thereon and set the plate down in front of Phineas. "Eat."

He began munching immediately. "Oh! I nearly forget something," he said, his mouth full. "I followed up on your inquiry about that man, Temenos, the one the Venetian tracked down. I found the same information her people did. It appears this Dorian Temenos died in Portugal."

In the heat of the quest for Aphrodite, I had tried to shake off the news that my father was dead. Upon return to London, however, the mystery haunted me. I'd asked Phin to contact Celeste's order. They were pleased to help me and passed on all their information to Phineas. "How did he die?" I asked. I set down the tea, again joining him at the table.

"I've got a record of him arriving in Lisbon then his death record about six months later. No other details."

"Oh," was all I could think to say. I took a sip of tea. The news left me unsatisfied. "Nothing else about him?"

"Not yet. No family records. No work records. I can travel to Lisbon if you want."

I shook my head. Something told me it was time to leave well enough alone. "No, that's okay."

"I'll be passing through Southwark later this week. I'll inquire about the grave you'd asked about—the woman at the debtor's prison. You still want me to do that?"

I nodded then set the cup down. I pressed my fingertips against my forehead. My head had started to ache.

"You all right, Lil? You want me to bring you something mild?"

Yes, I did. "No, I can't." I opened my eyes and looked inside my cup. The tea leaves had fallen into the shape of the triskelion, the symbol painted on the balloon of the *Stargazer*.

"Don't let this bit with the *Stargazer* rattle you. You might love that ship, but to others, it's just a beautiful thing they want a piece of. They don't care about it the way you do."

I smiled at Phin and set my hand on his.

He squeezed my fingers. His hazel eyes twinkled. I knew the look all too well. More than once, Phineas and I had enjoyed too much herbal and woke up in bed together. "You still with the Italian?" he asked slyly.

"Yes," I said, patted his hand, then let him go. "Regardless, you are in serious need of a bath, and I don't like that moustache."

Phineas laughed. "I thought it made me look gentlemanly," he said, stroking the moustache. "You know, I've been wondering. Why, out of all of us, was old Salvatore the one to win you away from Byron? What made him so special?"

I grinned at him. "Get some rest and don't forget to come by the *Stargazer* tomorrow." I rose to leave.

"All right, Lily," he said with a laugh. He followed me to the door.

Outside, thunder rumbled. I grabbed my hat, adjusted my lily pin to ensure it was securely fastened, tossed it on, and headed outside.

"And shave off that moustache," I called to Phineas who was leaning against the door frame smoking his pipe. Grinning, he bowed ever-so-elegantly then went inside.

I walked away thinking about Phin's question. I'd never really seen what had happened between Sal, Byron, and me like that. In the end, I still cared deeply for Byron. I just wanted something more, something different . . . with Sal.

CHAPTER 3

THE AIR WAFTING OFF THE Thames was perfumed with the mix of factory spill and spring flowers. Trees along the river were bursting with blossoms and crisp green leaves. Overhead, thunder rumbled again. The clouds were dark and forbidding. I sighed. It didn't take a genius to figure out why someone would sabotage us, but I was still shocked and angry.

As I walked, I thought about the *Stargazer*. I would never forget the first time I saw her. Angus and I had been flying the *Deirdre* since Mr. Fletcher's death. In 1818, we raced in the British qualifying and made second place. We realized that our ship, not our crew, was what had held us back. We needed a faster machine. As the 1819 qualifying approached, we had leads on two racing airships, one in Paris and the other in Stuttgart. Angus, Pidge—our balloon man at the time—and I headed first to Paris.

The Paris transport towers, unlike the race towers, were situated on Île de la Cité, the small island in the Seine River running through Paris. On one end of the island the Cathedral de Notre Dame stretched to the heavens. On the other end were more bawd houses, opium dens, and taverns than an opium eater like me could have ever asked for. The joke was that you could sin on one end of the island then repent on the other. I never made it to the Cathedral.

We'd arrived in Paris very late only to discover the ship vendor was even later than we were. Pidge stayed on the *Deirdre* to get some rest. Angus and I headed to the taverns below to look for trouble. It was easy to find, and it had a name: Lord Byron.

I had just returned from the opium den when Byron and his entourage entered Le Blonde Sale, The Dirty Blonde. The tavern was a dark, smoke-filled place that reeked of stale ale. Lit by just a few lamps, the space glowed with soft orange light. The noisy tavern erupted into a cheer when Byron walked into the room.

"Who is that?" I asked Angus as we both strained to get a look.

"Bloody hell, that's Lord Byron," Angus replied then whistled at the bartender to pour us another drink.

Lord Byron. There wasn't a woman alive who didn't know his name and reputation. Byron, a famous poet and a scandalous lover, was living in self-imposed exile abroad. I'd never seen him in person. I gazed through the crowd to get a look. Through my opium haze, I saw he was exactly as he had been described: heart-stopping. With dark curly hair, alabaster skin, red lips, and a laugh that filled the room, he made something in my stomach flutter. I wasn't the only one who responded to him. Every woman in the room, and many of the men, rushed to the door to meet him, to touch him, to be near him.

The bartender set the shots before us. I turned away from the crowd that thronged around the poet.

"What, aren't you going to gush all over him too?" Angus asked.

I lifted my drink and motioned for Angus to do the same. "One. Two. Three!" Angus and I drank. I downed the harsh liquor in one long swallow. It burned. I set the empty glass down. "No, I'm not."

"Why lassie, I'm surprised," Angus teased.

"There is only one way to get the attention of man like that."

Angus raised an eyebrow at me.

"Ignore him," I explained with a wicked grin. "Let's go."

"Wait, what?"

"Come on," I said and headed toward the door. As we passed Byron, I could see he was very drunk, maybe more drunk than me. And I didn't like the looks of the people who surrounded him. They looked little better than thieves and common street whores. Byron, however, seemed like he was having fun. I paused at the door to hold it open for Angus. And then I waited just a moment longer. Byron turned and leveled his blue eyes on me.

I winked at him then left.

Once we got outside, Angus laughed loudly. "Aye, that should do it," he said, and we headed into the tavern across the street.

Inside, we found tables lined up side by side as pairs engaged in a drinking competition. The place was packed with spectators. Angus and I pushed through the crowd to get a look. One man downed a shot then slumped sideways to the floor. Half the crowd around him cheered, the other half of the room ruefully handed over their francs.

"Let's bet," I shouted to Angus over the noise of the crowd as they lined up the next pair.

"Which one?" Angus replied.

We sized up the next pair; a wiry French lad was about to take on Russian twice his size.

"The boy looks too mean to lose," I said.

With a nod, Angus agreed, and we threw in our bet for the Frenchman.

Up went the shots. Both men stayed upright. Again, they drank. The Russian downed his drink, rose inexplicably, then toppled over. Angus and I cheered, collected our winnings, then took a table off to the side. I ordered an absinthe, Angus ordered a scotch, and we settled in. We'd been there for less than fifteen minutes when the bawdy crowd that surrounded Byron rambled in, the poet at its center.

I sipped my drink and watched him. He scanned the room. When he spotted me, he smiled. I looked away, pretending I hadn't seen him.

"Oy, I almost pity him," Angus said with a laugh.

I grinned. I heard Byron order a round of drinks which helped to disperse the crowd around him. Out of the corner of my eye, I saw him cross the room.

"Here he comes," Angus said, never looking at Byron.

"Puis-je vous joindre?" Bryon asked politely.

Angus grinned then got up to go watch the drinking match. "If you want," I said, motioning nonchalantly to the empty seat. Several people from Byron's entourage attempted to join us, but Byron shooed them away.

"English?" Byron more stated than asked. "Well, that is a surprise."

A tavern girl arrived at our table with two absinthes. She heaved her breasts toward Byron, trying to catch his attention, but he ignored her. Ruffled, she set the drinks down and stalked away.

Byron prepared our drinks, pouring cold water over sugar, then pushed a drink toward me. "To the green fairy," he said as he lifted his glass, referring to the enchanted—and occasionally monstrous—hallucinogenic creature thought to be evoked by drinking absinthe.

I lifted the drink, and we tapped our glasses together: "To the green fairy. May she guide us into the unknown," I agreed with a grin.

I took a drink, set my glass down, then leveled my eyes on Byron. We made direct eye contact. While my head was swimming in a haze of opium and alcohol, the color of his blue eyes was strikingly vivid. They drew me in like a chain had snared my heart. For a moment, I think I stopped breathing. But it wasn't the flashing blue of his eyes that had so ensnared me. There was something beyond them, behind them, which spoke to me. It was like, in that single instance, I saw him as everyone else did then saw past the façade to the soul within him. A fragile, broken, yet dangerous man lived behind those eyes. I'd never experienced anything like it in my life.

Byron, too, took a deep breath. He looked away, trying to appear nonchalant. He fidgeted with his sleeve. "Do you know who I am?" he asked.

I smiled weakly and tried to look bored, but my hands were shaking. "Of course."

He liked my answer. "What's your name?" he asked, turning again toward me, leaning on the table. His eyes searched my face.

For a split second, I wanted to say Penelope, my true given name. The instinctive reaction startled me. "I'll leave that for you to figure out."

"Hmm," Byron mused then took a drink. "Let's have a match."

"A match?"

Byron smiled slyly then motioned to the drinking game. "If I can match you five drinks, or win you over, you will tell me your name."

I thought it over. I had a solid ten drinks still left in me before I was apt to kiss the floor. "Agreed. Of course, if you win me over, I won't be able to tell you."

Byron laughed. "This is true. Let's make it more interesting . . . if I can match you or beat you by ten drinks, you'll owe me a kiss."

I looked over at Angus who, despite the fact that he was looking away from us, seemingly watching the game, was hearing every word. I waited for him to look back at me. He didn't, but he nodded.

"Agreed again."

"All right," Byron said with a grin, pounding his fist on the table, then called to the barkeep: "Nouveaux joueurs!"

The tavern erupted into a cheer.

Byron and I took seats across from one another and the barkeep poured five shots.

"Are you ready, Mademoiselle?" Byron asked me.

"Are you?"

Byron laughed.

"Santé," Byron said, toasting me, then tossed back his drink. I matched him drink for drink until the fourth shot. Byron slowed a little then looked me over, assessing me. "You can tell me now. You don't have to push yourself."

I laughed, picked up the drink, and downed it.

Byron grinned and matched me.

The crowd around us booed. It was a draw.

"Well?" Byron asked, arching an eyebrow at me.

"Lily," I replied.

"Lily? Hmm. Bonjour, sweet Lily. I'm George," he said then took my hand, daintily kissing it.

Beside me, Angus chuckled.

I grinned at Byron as the bartender set out five more shots.

"You do recall we've got some actual business to attend to tonight," Angus whispered in my ear. "It might be nice if you weren't out stone cold."

"I'm good," I replied.

Angus shook his head, but he was smiling.

"Now, for a taste of those lips," Byron said. "Cheers, Lily," he called and drank the first drink.

I matched him and drank the second as well.

Byron laughed, picked up his second glass, and drank.

The crowd around Byron cheered.

I picked up the third glass. I could handle it, but after one more, things would start going downhill.

Both Angus and I knew it. I smiled at Byron then drank.

"Bloody hell, the girl is more liquor than woman. Cheers to Lil-" Byron began, standing to toast me, but then his legs went out from under him. Down he went. His entourage, laughing loudly, caught him and dragged him to a chair along the wall where they propped him up.

"He's out," one of them shouted with a laugh.

Again, the laughing patrons exchanged francs. Many of them clapped me on the back in congratulations.

"Just in time too. I had to guess which one was the full glass last time," I told Angus as I settled the tab. I looked back at Byron who was surrounded by a crowd of noisy revelers. I smiled. He was snoozing peacefully propped against the wall. He'd have a hell of a headache when he woke.

Angus and I left the tavern and headed toward the towers. It was already after midnight. When we got to the guard post, they told us the vendor had arrived and was waiting for us on his ship.

"Christ, I can barely see straight," Angus said with a laugh as we made our way down the platform, a guard leading the way.

"Here you are, Mademoiselle. Monsieur Robert?" the guard called.

To my great shock, we had stopped beside a bulky old tub no better than the *Iphigenia*, the ship I'd grown up on. Monsieur Robert, the vendor, came to the ship's rail to greet us.

"What? What the hell is this?" I growled.

"Mademoiselle, I am sorry. The racing ship was sold in Toulouse. But this is a fine old ship. Very sturdy. I thought, perhaps, I could interest you in this vessel?"

"Oh, piss off!" Angus swore at him. "I should bust your teeth in for wasting our time."

"But Monsieur," Monsieur Robert protested.

Enraged, I called to mind the best French curse words Nicolette, my adoptive sister, had ever taught me, and told Monsieur Robert what I thought of him. When I was done, the vendor stood, pale and still as a stone, grasping the rail of his floating bathtub.

"Let's go," I told Angus who was laughing so hard his eyes watered.

"Christ, Lily. What did you do, curse his family line? I think he shit himself."

"Something like that," I replied, feeling a bit sorry for my words after the fact.

Depressed that we were no better off than before we'd come to Paris, Angus and I headed back to the taverns where he hoped to get one last drink, and I wanted one last smoke, before we went back to the *Deirdre*. We'd leave for Stuttgart that night. We didn't want to be late again.

"We'll have better luck next time," I reassured Angus.

"I sure as hell hope so, otherwise we'll be ferrying the circuit for another year."

As we crossed the street, we heard a scuffle in the alley. A small group of people were working over a tall man they had pressed against a building, turning out his pockets and knocking him hard in the gut.

"Keep walking," Angus whispered.

Something about the scene drew my attention. I realized that the crowd was the same I'd seen in the tavern clustered around Byron, and the man taking the pummeling was Lord Byron himself.

"Hey! You bloody rats, lay off," I yelled at them.

"Lily!" Angus scolded.

"That's Byron," I whispered harshly.

"It's not our business."

"Don't tell me that you, a Scot yourself, will leave a descendant of Scottish Lairds in a ditch in Paris to be robbed and beaten by thieves!"

"You had to bring that up, did you?" Angus grumbled at me. "All right. Bugger off you scoundrels," Angus yelled at them as he pulled his sidearm from his vest.

The minute the crowd saw the gun, they scattered. Moments later, Angus and I were standing over a bloodied and unconscious Lord Byron.

"What the hell are we supposed to do now?" Angus asked.

I shrugged. "Take him with us. We can drop him off in Stuttgart."

"What!"

"Well, we can't just leave him here. He's out cold. When he wakes up, he can catch a transport back to wherever he's supposed to be."

"He probably has people looking for him. Not to mention, he doesn't exactly have the reputation as the grateful type," Angus grumbled.

I looked down at Byron. Something about what I'd seen in his eyes made me think otherwise. "I'm not going to leave him here. Take him by the arms. I'll grab his legs."

"Christ," Angus swore.

And with a heave, we hauled Byron back to the *Deirdre*.

"Who is that?" Pidge had asked sleepily, rubbing his hand through his thin white hair, as Angus and I dumped Byron into my hammock.

"Lord Byron," Angus grumbled as he tried to catch his breath. "Whew. He needs to drop a few stones."

Pidge laughed. "Caught a buck in rut, did you, Lily? What the hell are we going to do with him?"

"That's what I asked," Angus grumbled.

"Let him to sober up," I replied. "Let's anchors aweigh for Stuttgart. The Paris ship was a bust. Let's haul it to Württemberg before someone cuts in on us again."

"You could have let me sleep another hour," Pidge said with a yawn as he climbed into the burner basket.

"And you two smell like you've been fished out of a liquor barrel."

"That's Byron," Angus said with a laugh then headed below deck.

I untethered the *Deirdre* and maneuvered the ship out of port. We'd make Stuttgart in the Kingdom of Württemberg before morning light. Setting the coordinates on the ship, I turned the ship east and headed across country. Cruising, unlike racing, was easy. As long as you kept the ship on her bearing, an eye on the clouds, and stayed on the lookout for pirates, there was little to distract you. I ran with only two lanterns burning. To avoid pirates, it paid to cruise quickly and without too much flash.

We sailed over the French countryside. The moon was nearly full, and there was little cloud cover. The stars overhead twinkled brightly. The moonlight above the rare cloud wisps cast long shadows on the ground below. The rivers and small ponds glistened with silver light. I locked the wheel and went to look over the side of the ship. Though it was a beautiful night, there was a chill in the air.

"You got your coat, Pidge?" I called up to the balloon basket.

"Aye, Lily, and some rum," he said with a laugh.

I chuckled and pulled my coat from the storage bin. I cast an eye back toward Byron whose loose white shirt ruffled in the breeze. I also pulled a thick blanket from the locker and went to the hammock. I lay the heavy blanket over Byron, tucking it around his body. When I moved to adjust his arms, his eyes fluttered open for a moment. He gazed wistfully at me, smiled, then closed his eyes again. I laughed, shook my head, then pulled the blanket up to his chin.

I went back to the wheelstand. It was turning out to be an interesting night. Keeping my eye on the instruments, I guided the ship over the French border and into the Kingdom of Württemberg. Just a few hours later we were passing over the northern end of the Black Forest; we'd soon be in Stuttgart.

Taking a break, I pulled out my tobacco pipe. I hoped the tobacco would help me clear my head a little. My back against the wheelstand, I lit the pipe and smoked as I stared up at the stars through my spyglass. They twinkled brightly in the last of the night's sky.

"Stargazer."

The sound of another voice startled me. I lowered the spyglass to find Byron sitting up in the hammock looking at me.

"Pardon?"

"You're a stargazer," he said then motioned to the stars overhead. "By the by, where am I?" he asked as he rubbed his temples.

"You're aboard the *Deirdre*."

"Have you abducted me?" he asked with a grin.

I smiled. "Rescued, more like. We plucked you out of a ditch."

"That was kind of you. Where are we headed?"

"Stuttgart."

"Whatever for?"

Given that I wasn't prone to sharing the personal details of my life, I looked Byron over and considered my answer. Still, I said, "I'm after a new ship."

"Why?"

"We ran second in the British qualifying last year. This year we will win."

"The airship races?"

I nodded.

"Lily, Stuttgart towers," Pidge called.

I rose, smiled at Byron, then took the wheel. I rang the galley. "Angus! Docking! Wake up!" I called, stomping on the deck.

After a moment, the propeller eased.

In the dim, pre-dawn light, I eyed the lights on the airship towers.

"Spots open on the south end," Pidge called.

I lifted my spyglass and looked. Byron, wrapped in my blanket, came up beside me. He stared at the towers.

I handed him the spyglass and grabbed the wheel, turning it ever-so-slightly starboard.

"Up a bit, Pidge," I called. "Five percent or so." The burner heaved and the balloon lifted. We coasted toward the dock.

"*You* piloted the ship that placed second in qualifying?" Byron asked as he stared through the spyglass toward the towers.

"Yes."

He lowered the glass and looked down at me. Out of the corner of my eye, I saw him smile.

The crew in Stuttgart waved us in. With a few wheel turns, I brought the *Deirdre* to anchor in the southern tower.

Angus climbed out of the galley, and we went about anchoring the ship while Pidge debarked to go talk with the stationmaster. Byron, who had dropped the blanket and was making an attempt at tidying himself up, watched with fascination.

After we were done, Angus turned to Byron. "Good morning, Lord Byron," Angus said, sticking out his hand. "We were never properly introduced. Angus MacArthur."

"MacArthur? I understand I owe you thanks, brother."

"Well, you can't just go and leave a fellow Scot lying in a ditch in Paris," Angus said, winking at me.

"Thankfully, apparently not," Byron replied.

Pidge returned with the stationmaster and a stout looking man who was, no doubt, the airship vendor. Neither man spoke a word of English, but Pidge, whose mother hailed originally from Berlin, managed the conversation.

"The racer is here, Lily. By god, wait until you see!" Pidge exclaimed excitedly.

The vendor, Herr Weber, eyed the *Deirdre* over, nodded politely to us, then motioned for us to come along. Pidge and Herr Weber talked seriously as we followed behind.

"Remind me, Lily, how old is the *Deirdre*? When was she built?" Pidge asked me.

"1814. She's four . . . she's only had one other owner besides me," I replied.

Angus looked at me but said nothing. There was no need to get into the details of how I had come to own her.

We crossed onto the eastern platform just as the sun rose above the horizon. I scanned the docking bays but saw nothing that looked like a racing ship. I started to feel depressed. It would be the same scene as in Paris all over again. We headed down a platform toward a whale of a boat. Dammit! I had it in my mind to dig in my heels and not take another step forward when the first rays of sun glimmered brightly off the timbers of a nearby ship. I winced.

"God," I heard Angus gasp.

When I opened my eyes again, I saw that Angus had taken a few steps forward and was staring, mouth open, at the docking bay. I followed his gaze, again wincing in the sunlight. There, her honey-colored timbers gleaming, was the most beautiful racing ship I'd ever seen. She was magnificent.

"Try not to look so impressed," Byron whispered in my ear. "It worked on me."

I smiled and looked up at him. He dropped his arm around my shoulder, filling my senses with his sweet scent of orange blossom and patchouli. We went forward to look at the racing ship. With Byron's arm around me and the ship of my dreams before me, I felt like I was on fire.

Herr Weber invited us aboard the racer. When I touched the ship, I felt a jolt. She was perfect. She was lightweight, built tight, and had the most advanced propeller system available. Even the balloon burners were retooled to burn more efficiently. She was perfect. Not only would we be able to place in the qualifying, but this ship could be a contender in the Prix.

Keeping Byron's suggestion in mind, I casually asked Pidge to inquire what Herr Weber wanted for the ship. I tried not to let on I'd give my right hand for it. Herr Weber, who seemed to be good at this game, inquired if we were interested in considering the *Deirdre* in the transaction. Of course we were, because without the trade, the three of us had little by way of coin. Though none of us had eaten a proper meal in the last year for sake of saving all our fare money, the earnings we had were not impressive. When Weber named his price, I nearly burst into tears. It was twice what we had in coin. Pidge, however, impressed me.

He laughed kindly, clapped Herr Weber on the shoulder, and tried again.

Byron watched the exchange with interest. I stood, fretting, as I listened to Pidge and Herr Weber while Angus crawled all over the racer. He returned midway through the negotiations with his assessment.

"Her beams aren't nearly as tight as they should be, and she has galley parts that need replaced to meet our specifications. She's running illegal bits we'll need to trim out. She's not as good as she looks," Angus said with a frown, Pidge translating.

Herr Weber looked surprised. He scowled as he reconsidered.

Byron turned to Angus and asked him a question in a Gaelic dialect I recognized but didn't understand. When Angus answered him, Byron nodded but kept a straight face. I looked from Angus, whose face gave away nothing, back to Byron. A small glimpse into Byron's eyes told me that Angus had lied. I looked away.

Herr Weber considered thoughtfully, gave me a hard look, then asked Pidge a question.

Pidge smiled at me then nodded.

I worried.

Herr Weber began talking very quickly.

Pidge turned toward us. "We can't quite come to terms on price," he said with a shake of the head. "He wants more than we have, the *Dierdre* included, but he has daughters Lily's age and likes that Lily is going to pilot the ship. He is a believer in fortune, so he'll give us a shot. He says that if we can best him in a game of cards, he'll make the deal."

"Based on a game of cards?" I asked, aghast.

Pidge nodded.

Herr Weber rubbed his hands together, his eyes glinting with a card player's passion.

I looked at Angus. In truth, I was an opium eater and an alcoholic, and Angus was just as much of a drunk as me, but neither of us were card players. Pidge, who went to church on Sundays, was about as straight as they came. It was over.

"Let's play," Byron said.

I looked up at him.

"It's as easy as rhyming," Byron told me with a shrug.

Herr Weber smiled, and we headed to the guard station. The stationmaster cleared a table for Byron and Herr Weber, and soon the cards were being dealt. I could tell from the impressions on the faces of the stationmaster and the guards that they thought we were in for a trouncing. Apparently, in Stuttgart, Byron was not yet famous.

The two men sat across from one another, both with serious expressions on their faces. I tried to read Herr Weber. He looked like he was settling in for a battle. His cheeks were flushed with excitement. I dared not look at Byron, knowing that if I read him, others might be able to read me. I waited. Three exchanges in, Byron called. Herr Weber looked shocked when Byron lay down an unbeatable hand.

Just like that, it was over.

Herr Weber, who looked like he was trying to decide whether or not to be angry or to laugh, ultimately laughed out loud. The man reached across the table and shook Byron's hand. Byron had won us the ship.

CHAPTER 4

WHEN I ARRIVED AT THE large, two-story brick building overlooking the Thames, workmen were hanging a sign above the door: *The Daedalus Company.* I looked through the windows to see Sal making his way down an aisle on the factory floor. I felt guilty. I'd been lost in my memories of the *Stargazer* and Byron. It seemed unfair to Sal. He was my life now; Byron was my past.

I gazed up at the sign. On it was the image of Daedalus soaring with his tinkered wings spread wide. I smiled. The man I loved was about to become very wealthy. My stunt in Paris at the 1823 World Grand Prix had brought acclaim, not only to the *Stargazer's* crew, but to Sal. A French tinker experimenting with a heliography device managed to photograph my leap from the *Stargazer*, parachute fully launched. The image was re-interpreted and printed as an engraving in every American and European newspaper. The minute everyone realized that there was a reliable parachute to be purchased, they wanted one. Sal found himself in the fortunate position of having far more work than he could ever manage on his own. When the race league decided to make it mandatory for all racers to have a parachute, Sal went from being a tinker to being a businessman. I ducked under the sign and entered the factory.

"Sal?" I called.

He turned and smiled at me. His small, round glasses were pushed up on his head. He carried a bundle of rope over one shoulder and a fist full of papers. "Ahh, here is my Lily."

"How is it coming?" I wrapped my arms around him, pressing my head against his chest. Amongst all the chaos of the day, this was a moment of peace.

Deliverymen were everywhere. Workers were uncrating equipment and stowing supplies. Sal had hired ten young men and three young ladies to apprentice under him. They were excited. I didn't blame them. Unlike most factory owners, Sal promised his apprentices both an education and payment for their services. Indenturing of apprentices without pay, which was a common practice and a fate I had suffered under the guise of adoption, was something Sal and I both found repugnant. Sal was determined, in a fatherly sort of way, to pass on his knowledge. The apprentices were lucky, and they knew it. The gusto with which they worked showed their appreciation. They only stopped when they saw me come in. They began whispering excitedly.

"Excellent. The rolls of silk just arrived from the Orient," Sal said, motioning to a row of large crates sitting on the floor. "Mr. Duncan's shipment of sewing machines came yesterday, and we've just finished setting up the tables for the girls," he said, motioning toward one corner of the workshop.

The young ladies Sal employed would work only in part on the parachutes. At my urging, Sal decided to market another of his ingenious inventions: the clockwork bodice, an easily removed undergarment Byron once highly admired on—and off—of me. Sal's design, however, needed a female touch, which the seamstresses could provide. The girls, who were setting up their stations, smiled and waved at me.

"They've just finished the work upstairs. Would you like to see?" Sal asked carefully.

Neither he nor I were sure how I'd respond. After the race, I sold my flat on Hart Street and had been bouncing between staying with the boys, on the *Stargazer*, and with Sal at his flat near Hungerford Market, which was really too small for us both. When Sal suggested that the space above the factory be transformed into *our* home, I'd only trepidatiously agreed. Part of me knew that if I wanted to make this work, I needed to try to have a normal relationship.

But more and more, I got the sense that Sal was starting to see me as his future wife—and maybe even the mother of his children. The fatherly looks he gave his apprentices and the cozy way he handled me was starting to make me feel a bit edgy.

I pulled back from our embrace and looked at him as steadily as I could. "Sure, let's take a look."

Sal set down his equipment, signaled to Henry, the eldest of the apprentices, and we headed upstairs. Pushing open the trap door, Sal took my hand and helped me up.

The second floor of the factory had tall, windows on all sides. The space, save the private bath, was entirely open. The layout would have scandalized the typical housewife. We had furnished a parlor space, dining space, workspace, and our bedroom in separate areas. Sal had purchased some dressing screens for our bedroom. He'd also won us an enormous bed at auction. The four-poster canopy bed had once belonged to a noble family. Such a regal piece of furniture looked funny in such an odd space but not bad.

"Everything is in working order, livable," Sal told me.

I scanned the space. Was this really my home? This was what I wanted, wasn't it? It was, after all, what I had chosen. I went to the window and looked out. I could see the airship towers where the damaged *Stargazer* was docked. I touched the glass.

"If you are having second thoughts . . ."

"No," I replied absently. I wasn't, was I? "I'll bring my things over. We can sleep here tonight," I said then paused. I could feel his eyes wandering over me. "It's not that," I said, turning to him, strengthening my stance. "We've had some bad luck on the *Stargazer*," I said then explained to Sal what had happened.

"I'll ask Henry to mind things here," Sal said after I'd relayed the situation. "I need to go back to my stall at Hungerford and pick up some parts. With so much damage, it might be a good time to sketch a better design."

"You have an idea?"

Sal nodded. "I've been considering one for a while now. I think there is a way to get better rotation . . . well, we can discuss it later. I have some drawings at the workshop. What time is the qualifying meeting?"

"Seven."

Sal wrapped his arms around my waist. "You'll be fine, my Lily. We'll have you racing again in no time," he whispered in my ear.

I wanted to believe him, yet something within me ached, and I couldn't shake the feeling. I looked back at the towers. The clouds overhead were dark, and rain had started to fall.

CHAPTER 5

ANGUS, JESSUP, SAL, AND I stood outside the door of *The Lancelot Club*, in the rain, waiting for permission to join the other league teams. We were there for two things: news about the upcoming British qualifying race and to learn which cities would be hosting the 1824 World Grand Prix. The longer I stood in the rain, however, the more annoyed I was getting. Given we had to take a Thames ferry to Chelsea rather than just holding the meeting near the towers, I was about to lose my patience. I was far less tolerant than I had been with laudanum pumping through my body. It was ridiculous that we were made to wait. Everyone knew who we were.

"Maybe we should have brought the '23 World Grand Prix cup," Jessup grumbled.

"Formality, friend. You Brits have a knack for formality," Sal joked.

"You suppose we ought to queue up?" Jessup replied.

Sal grinned.

Neither Angus nor I were laughing. Considering we were both already ready to pummel someone for the condition the *Stargazer* was in, one more slight felt like one more too many.

"Miss Stargazer, so sorry to make your team wait. The league chairman has permitted your entry," the doorman finally said.

"What a fucking joke," Angus swore as he pushed past.

Sal nodded politely, Jessup following behind him.

"Sorry, Lily," the doorman whispered under his breath as I passed by.

I smiled reassuringly at him.

We were led to a large meeting room at the back of the club. Every team in the British Racing League was already assembled. I felt like I was in a den of wolves. Every eye turned to us; some looked on with envy, some with anger, and a scant few with pride. Julius Grant, his team, and his sponsors were all there. Lord D and his team, all wearing fashionable—and matching—suits, had also assembled. Other pilots and their peerage or company backers also filled the room. I saw so many new faces in the crowd. Money, it seemed, was buying entrance for pilots better suited to polo.

There were only two other teams in the room from our slice of society: the commoner air jockey. Last year, the British Racing League had enacted a heavy fee for entrance into the club. With Byron's help, we'd had enough to make it in, but many others who were better pilots than most of the moneymen in the room could not afford to join. The new rules rendered them too poor to race. I didn't like the direction things were headed.

The air was thick with cigar smoke, and everyone was drinking. A footman offered us drinks from a silver serving tray. Angus took two. Jessup joined him. Sal, out of consideration, passed. I knew I dare not touch a drop, but my mouth watered at the thought.

"All right, racers. With Stargazer's team here, we are all accounted for. Take a seat, one and all," the British league chairman called.

We took a seat in the very back with the teams for the *Mary Stewart* and the *Falstaff*.

"Hey Bigsby," I whispered to the pilot of the *Falstaff*, "where is Mandy?"

"Out," Bigsby replied in a whisper. "Didn't you hear? The *Ruby* burned."

"What? When?" Angus asked.

"Two days back."

Jessup leaned toward Bigsby. "How?"

Bigsby shrugged. "Accident, I guess."

We all looked at one another. Mandy was the only other female pilot in the British racing league.

Sal took out a pen and journal and began writing. Angus checked his gun. Even I'd brought my sidearm tonight. It was safely stowed inside my vest. I scanned the room. Grant's head was bowed, but his eyes, hiding under a lock of dark hair, were fixed on me. He smiled, his large lips pulling taut across his small face. The expression looked like it pained him. I wanted to punch him in the mouth. I looked away.

"Racers, welcome, welcome!" the British league chairman called excitedly from the front of the room. I noticed that his emerald green suit was the same shade of green as the rug. "Let's get down to business, shall we? As you know, the 1824 British qualifying race will be held May 1st. We've planned special May Day events in Edinburgh and London as the race kicks off and closes. This year we've planned a special fireworks display . . ."

Then he went on about all the festivities and pageantry we could expect on British qualifying day, but I wasn't really listening. Instead, I looked around. Who were all the new faces? Several of them sneaked a glance at me. I could practically feel the target on me.

"Before we talk about this year's World Grand Prix," the chairman went on, "I have some exciting news about changes that will be enacted next year for the 1825 races, including the 1825 British qualifying! Big news, my friends, big news."

The room erupted in excited whispers.

"Calm. Calm. But this is exciting news, to say the least. We've had word that in the 1825 races, including qualifying trials, racers will be permitted to use airships with double propulsion!"

Several teams in the front of the room rose to their feet, cheering, including Lord D's team. Grant spoke in a quiet huddle with his sponsors then smiled smugly. If your team had a lot of money, this was great news. We were finally going to be able to use the same designs that the airship pirates leveraged.

I could feel the blood leaving my cheeks. Around me, the *Mary Stewart's* and *Falstaff's* teams shrunk in their seats. The reality was that if you wanted to race next year, even in qualifying, you would need a new ship.

Angus and Jessup exchanged glances.

Sal tapped his pen against his paper. "I have a plan," he had written.

I was a World Champion. I had a sponsor. If I needed corporate backing, I could elicit it. But I didn't want it. What I wanted was for crews who flew airships every day, the real air jockeys, to race. Flying was not about money, it was about skill and love of the air. In one fell swoop, the league had essentially ensured that no commoner would ever race again.

"Ladies and gentlemen, we also have some news about this year's World Grand Prix. The British team who wins the 1824 qualifying will have a massive, wonderful, exciting challenge at hand. Pay close attention here. Unlike the usual World Grand Prix races which have been, historically, set in four countries, the 1824 World Grand Prix racers, including one winning team in this room, will compete in an around-the-world race!"

This time, the room was stunned silent. Such a race was dangerous beyond measure: rough weather, uncharted lands, pirates, and god-only-knows what else. I quickly thought about what the flight path might even look like. I had no doubt in my mind that we would win qualifying, that we would take the British slot in the World Grand Prix, but now I knew we were going to be up for a dangerous challenge. We could handle it. No, we could win it, but still. Why had they changed the scope of the race so dramatically?

I looked from Angus to Jessup.

"Did he just say what I think he said?" Jessup asked.

"Aye, brother," Angus said in a low tone. Angus' eyes met mine. We both knew this meant trouble. "Oy," Angus called to the chairman with a whistle, "whose bloody idea was that?"

Everyone in the room looked at us. From their expressions, it seemed that suddenly winning the British slot in the 1824 World Grand Prix was a lot less appealing to the polo players in the room.

The chairman shifted uncomfortably. "Not sure, Angus. There was some rumbling about a new World Grand Prix sponsor, but nothing concrete," he said then quickly shifted the conversation to the standard race regulations for the upcoming British qualifying.

I sighed. "Well, we've never seen Kiev," I told my crew.

Angus grunted in assent.

Jessup groaned sarcastically. "Wonderful."

"What's navigating a single planet to a girl who can out-riddle the stars?" Sal whispered in my ear, but I also noticed that he had put his arm protectively around me.

"If I recall correctly, you were responsible for much of the riddle solving," I whispered back.

Sal reached out and touched my cheek. "I was motivated."

I chuckled.

The chairman went on and on until he realized, at last, that almost everyone in the room was bored and anxious to talk about the announcements. "All right, racers. Formality is closed. We are expecting further details about the 1824 World Grand Prix flight path; they've promise the British league they will provide our representative a detailed guide. That is all the information I have for now. Any questions?"

No one dared ask out of fear of the length and breadth of an answer.

"Good, good. Please, enjoy the rest of the night. Drinks are courtesy of the club!"

"Fuck this place. Let's go," Angus said, echoing exactly what I was thinking.

Bigsby turned to us. "Let's head back to the towers. Want to meet at Rose's Hopper?"

We agreed then rose to leave. I eyed the room on my way out. Grant was crossing the room toward me. I saw his thin frame weaving in and out of the crowd.

"Lily?" he called.

I pretended I had not heard him.

"Lily?" he called again.

I stopped. "What do you want, Julius?"

"You aren't leaving yet, are you? Why don't you stay and have a drink?" His upbeat tone and the sour, frowning expression on his face were entirely discordant.

"Sorry, we've got other issues to attend to."

"Very well. But . . . issues? I do hope everything is all right with the *Stargazer*? I heard about Mandy's ship . . ."

Angus, Jessup, Sal and I all turned and looked at him. In that single moment, it appeared that Grant realized he'd said too much. He tried to smile innocently, but his over-arching eyebrows bespoke his anxiety. Angus took a step forward, but Sal motioned him to stand back.

I took Grant by the arm and leaned into his ear. "When we burn past you in qualifying, you'll see that nothing and no one can touch us, no matter what," I said then let him go. "Now, go have a nice night," I added, patting him on the cheek condescendingly, then left.

CHAPTER 6

WE WERE STILL TALKING ABOUT the exchange with Grant as we walked down the platform toward the *Stargazer*. Angus, Jessup, and I wanted to grab our gear before meeting Bigsby and the others at the tavern. It had been an ill-omened day. From the sabotage of the *Stargazer* to the 1824 route change to the 1825 switch to double propulsion, there was so much to discuss.

"Grant is worthy of ridicule, but if he is dangerous enough to be involved in the sabotage of the *Stargazer*, there is no telling what else he might try," Sal cautioned.

"You're right, which is why we're going to call in the last chip we have to get this mess rectified," I replied.

"What do you mean, Lil?" Jessup asked.

"Tomorrow, we will petition for a meeting with his majesty."

"With King Georgie?" Jessup replied.

"How many times have we been told how proud King George is of our team? How proud he is that we won the World Grand Prix? How proud he is of my 'noble spirit?' Well, let's see how true the rumors are. If he is as proud as everyone keeps telling us he is, then who better to put a stamp of approval on us? After that, we're untouchable. And if I can run my mouth the way I hope, maybe we can even get some league changes put back to right," I explained.

"Are you sure you aren't drunk?" Jessup asked.

"I wish."

"It's a good idea," Angus said with a nod. "King George is pigheaded enough to tell everyone to sod off just for the sake of doing so. And Lily is good enough looking to convince him."

"Was that a compliment?" I asked with a laugh.

As we neared the *Stargazer*, however, we noticed that a small group had assembled on the platform nearby. Two of the tower guards were there, the stationmaster, and a fourth man who I could not quite make out.

"Bloody hell," Jessup grumbled. "Now what?"

We picked up our pace and headed toward the ship. My eyes assessed every curve of the *Stargazer* as I made my way toward her. She looked okay. There was no sign of fire or damage. I couldn't see anything wrong, yet my stomach churned all the same, and my hands started to shake. The guards had seen us approaching. They turned to us.

"Lily," Sal whispered.

A small man pushed through the guards. At once, I recognized Byron's secretary. I smiled when I saw him and took a step toward him. I scanned the platform for Byron's ship. I saw a small, sleek vessel anchored nearby. I looked back at the secretary. The usually placid man looked hollow in the cheeks, pale, and the lines on his forehead were deeply furrowed.

"Isn't that Byron's man?" Jessup asked Angus.

"Wait," Angus said, which I thought was an odd reply.

"Lily," Sal said again, his voice filled with worry.

I took two more steps toward the secretary who moved in tandem toward me. He shifted uncomfortably. He wouldn't meet my eyes. His hands were shaking visibly.

My fingers began to tingle as the blood left them. I tried to take a deep breath, but I couldn't. My head started to feel very light.

"Miss Stargazer, I need you to come with me at once. Lord Byron . . . Lord Byron is dying. I was dispatched from Missolonghi with immediacy to fetch you. My Lord has been asking repeatedly for you. We don't expect him to live out the week."

"LILY," SAL WHISPERED CALMLY. MY eyes were closed. From the soft rocking feeling, I knew I was on the *Stargazer*. A cool cloth stroked my cheek. I caught Sal's sandalwood scent in the fabric. I opened my eyes. Sal was holding me against his chest as he knelt on the deck of the *Stargazer*. Jessup, Angus, and Byron's secretary were looking at me.

"You fainted," Angus told me.

I sat up. My head was bursting, but it was nothing compared to the sharp pain that had gripped my heart. I grabbed the secretary's coat sleeve, startling him. "What happened?"

"Lord Byron was sick in the winter, as you no doubt knew," the secretary said. He was wrong. I hadn't known. I hadn't known. Why hadn't I known? "He never made a full recovery. A few weeks back, he was caught in a rainstorm and took fever. He has not responded to the treatments prescribed to him. He's fading."

He could be dead before I got there. I stood.

"Easy," Sal said.

My head was still spinning. "I . . . but the *Stargazer* . . . Grant . . ." I said, turning to Angus.

"Go on. We'll be all right. Duncan will come, Phineas will snoop it out . . . and we'll see King George when you get back," Angus said.

Jessup was looking from Angus to Sal and back to me.

I took Sal's hand. I wouldn't dare a repeat of the confusion we'd had in Athens. "Sal," I began, but he stopped me.

"I will not deny a man his dying wish."

"Salvatore." I reached up and touched his cheek.

"Please, Miss Stargazer, we must make haste. The pilot is ready," the secretary said.

I felt like I was sleep walking as I debarked the *Stargazer* and headed across the platform to the small ship anchored there.

Angus leaned across the rail of the small ship separating us and pulled me into a tight hug, crushing me in his arms. "Tell him . . . thank him for me, thank him for all he's done for us. No other person in this world ever put their faith in us the way he did. Tell him thank you. And Lily, don't lose yourself," Angus whispered. I was surprised when I saw him wipe away a tear.

The pilot pulled up the anchors, and the propeller clicked on. The balloon started to fill with hot air, and with a heave, the small ship lifted out of the dock. I lifted my hand to wave to Sal. He looked worried, but he tried to smile. In that single moment, I remembered that tonight Sal and I had planned to sleep in our home together—our new home—like the couple that we were supposed to be. Instead, I was on my way back to Byron.

CHAPTER 7

I SAT IN SILENCE AT the prow of Byron's private ship, the *Aster*, as it flew quickly across the English Channel. Byron's secretary paced the deck. Part of me told me to distract myself, to talk to the captain about the flight plans for the ship, to ask her speed, to look at her galley. But in the end, I didn't move.

"When can we expect to make port?" was the only thing I asked.

The captain looked at me in surprise, as if I should have known the answer. Maybe I should have, but I couldn't think clearly. All the concerns that had been weighing so heavily on my mind fled like rats. I felt shocked to my core. My mind and body felt numb.

"We're thirty hours out, maybe less if we catch the wind. We'll need to stop to provision," the captain replied. His look had changed from surprise to sympathy.

I put my head down on the rail of the ship. What if I didn't make it in time? What if he died before I got there? Byron once told me the story of how he'd raced to his mother's deathbed only to miss her final moments by a few hours. It had wounded him deeply. If I was flying the *Stargazer*, I would make it. She wouldn't let him die without me.

BACK WHEN BYRON HAD LEARNED we were headed to Calais after he'd won us the racer in Stuttgart, he decided to fly with us rather than wait for a transport from, as he put it, the middle of nowhere. We shifted our gear from the *Deirdre* to the racer as fast as possible before Herr Weber decide he wanted more money than was agreed upon—a hand of cards won or not. In the end, fortune really was on our side. The ship was ours. I signed over the *Deirdre* using the name "Lily Fletcher" for the last time. It left me with a sense of finality. Once again, I buried an identity that did not suit me. When I signed my name to the racer, I signed only "Lily."

Angus, Pidge, Byron and I boarded the racer, and we began our preparations for departure.

"Wait!" Pidge called, turning from the basket ladder. "We can't fly her yet! She doesn't have a name. It's bad luck."

"Aye, you're right about that," Angus replied.

I held the wheel of the ship, its brass handles warm in the sunshine, and considered.

"She is the *Stargazer*, of course," Byron said as he pulled a bottle of laudanum from a pocket somewhere inside his pants and took two drops. He then pulled a small flask from the same hidden pocket.

"The *Stargazer*?" Angus mused.

"Hey, I like that. What do you think, Lily?" Pidge asked.

"Who am I to argue with a poet?"

"Shall we christen her properly?" Byron suggested. He came to the prow of the ship with his flask in hand.

We joined him.

"To the *Stargazer*," Byron said, "may she ever outrun the wind," he added and poured honey-colored liquor on the prow.

"To the *Stargazer!*" we cheered.

Byron passed around his flask, and we all toasted the ship. When the flask came to me, I took a sip and looked up at Byron. Was this really the man who had scandalized all of Britain with his wild ways? His reputation suggested that he might look to me for an in-kind thanks for his services, but his eyes told me a different story. The man behind those eyes was looking for something else.

I DIDN'T DEBARK WHEN THE *Aster* stopped in Zurich for provisions. The captain headed to the guard station while the crew prepared the *Aster* for the next leg of our trip. I stayed on the ship and waited impatiently while a storm brewed in my heart. I clung to the rail of the *Aster*. Below, I could make out the workshop of Master Vogt. My memories of the adventure in Knidos were still fresh. It was this route that had cemented Sal and me together. But as I retraced my steps back to Greece, I was not thinking about Sal, or Asclepius, or even Aphrodite. Now, the sole image in my mind was of Byron waving goodbye to me on the platform in Athens. Would that be my last memory of him? Would that be the last time I saw him alive? A single thought beat like a drum in my head: please don't let him die without me.

I PILOTED THE NEWLY-CHRISTENED *STARGAZER* out of Stuttgart and set a north-west course toward Calais. We would fly up the eastern border of France and reach the Calais towers by midnight. From Calais, Byron would be able to hop a transport to anywhere in

Europe. We were over the vineyards south of Reims when I decided that the ship was every bit as sturdy as promised. It was time to see what the *Stargazer* was made of.

I opened the hatch on the gear galley. The sound startled Byron who'd nodded off after we'd left Stuttgart. "Angus, let's stretch her legs a bit, shall we?" I called down.

"Christ, Lily, I thought you'd never ask," Angus replied.

"You ready, Pidge?" I called up.

"As I'll ever be."

"Now, for some real fun," I told Byron who suddenly looked very alert.

"Give it some lift," I called to Pidge. "About 10 percent. Let her run," I called to Angus, ringing the bell to the galley.

I watched the clouds. They were drifting west to east. Ahead, however, a wind was pushing the trees northerly. The propeller began to turn over hard. The balloon pulled us upward. The ship picked up speed. For a moment, she seemed like she was easing into it too slowly. Then the prop really began to turn, and she showed us what she was made of. The ship sped across the sky like she'd been flung from a slingshot. Suddenly, we were blasting through the crisp air.

"She's got some run on her!" Pidge yelled from above, laughing.

Byron, who had come to stand beside me, was smiling.

"Hold on," I told Byron then piloted the ship into the northern wind current above the trees.

The gust grabbed the back of the ship and heaved her forward with so much force that Byron lost his balance. I grabbed hold of him with one hand while I held the wheel with the other. I couldn't help but laugh out loud, Byron joining me. I cast a quick look up at him; his curly hair flew backward in the wind as he laughed.

"Amazing!" he yelled.

From below deck, I could hear Angus whooping loudly.

It was the fastest I'd ever flown. We shot so fast across the sky that I cast a worried glance up at the balloon, but the ship was just as tight as she seemed. Not one tether loosened or stretched. The ship was built for speed.

On the horizon ahead was a small hill that would disrupt the wind current. We were riding the shear. It would either mold to the shape of the land, pushing us up and over, or we would grind to a screeching halt as the current flattened. Judging by the size of the hill, I expected the wind to carry us over with a bump. It would be like flying up a ramp.

"Pidge, Angus, bump up ahead," I yelled.

Pidge looked out with his spyglass. "Hold on!"

As we neared the small hill, the wind shear pushed us from behind. I was right. It would be a jump. As the *Stargazer* rode the wind over the hill, she tipped up a bit at the prow. Then the airship moved with the wind, climbing the current. The Stargazer catapulted through the air.

Below deck, Angus yelled in excitement.

"Whooo!" Byron shouted, squeezing my shoulders excitedly, rocking me back and forth.

I grinned from ear to ear.

On the other side of the hill the land was flat. We dropped back into the normal west-east current. I rang the galley. The propeller dropped speed. The balloon took the weight of the ship, and we coasted. It was beautiful. We were flying fast, so fast, but easy and clean. The ship was a winner.

I started jumping up and down. Angus crawled out of the galley, and Pidge climbed down from the basket. They were hugging each other happily. Dizzy with excitement, I turned and planted a passionate kiss on Byron's red lips. He seemed startled but fell into it all the same, his wild excitement matching my own.

When I had let the passion out of me, I pulled away and screamed loudly, Angus and Pidge joining me. I grabbed Angus and Pidge, linking my arms in theirs, and rattled off a reel that they quickly joined:

Heigh-ho!
Sing heigh-ho!
Unto the green holly.

Most friendship is feigning, most loving mere folly.
Then, heigh-ho! The holly!
This life is most jolly.

Byron stood smiling at me. I grinned happily, knowing fortune was finally on my side.

IT WAS ALREADY AROUND NOON when I woke on the deck of the *Aster* with a pounding headache. Curled up alongside the rail, the secretary was still sleeping. Overhead, the balloonman looked like he was drifting. The *Aster* was still flying fast, but the captain looked like he was about to drop. I rose and stretched, joining the captain at the wheel.

"I can take over if you'd like to rest," I told him.

"It's all right, Lily. I can finish the trip."

"Where are we?" We were riding high aloft. The ground below was concealed by clouds.

"About two hours south of Pescara. We stopped there for just a bit. I didn't see any reason to wake you. We're following the Italian coast. We'll hop across the sea this evening and follow the Greek coast south to Missolonghi."

"Is the ship on heading?"

"It is."

"I can take the wheel. Just get a little sleep. I'll wake you if I need anything."

"Are you . . . are you sure you're okay?"

I nodded. I wasn't, but I hoped flying would help.

Reluctantly, the captain agreed. He let the balloonman and his galleyman know I had taken over then sat down along the rail. He was asleep within minutes. I pitied him. There was nothing worse than flying with the feeling that the hounds of hell are chasing you. Part of me hoped that somehow, with me at the helm, maybe I could coax a little more speed out of the *Aster*.

DURING THAT FIRST ENCOUNTER WITH Byron, I'd arrived in Calais with a mix of feelings. It was my own fault. I should have known better. Byron was a notorious womanizer whose erotic tastes had led him to self-imposed exile. Byron was the kind of man every mother warned her daughter about, but my mother had tried to drown me in a river, so I pretty much just ran on instinct. And his blue eyes haunted me with feelings I didn't understand.

He let me go easy, which further puzzled me. In Calais, he found a transport to Italy. I was still unsure what to say or how to thank him as I went with him to his transport ship.

"Lily . . . Lily Stargazer," he'd teased. "It was a memorable journey."

"Thank you, George. I don't know what else to say. I'm just so grateful."

Byron tapped the brim of my cap. Then, as if on second thought, he planted a knee-melting kiss on me. I dissolved into it. My senses imploded with the sweet taste of his lips, his scent of orange blossom and patchouli, and the feel of his strong hands pressing me tightly against his muscular body. When he finally pulled back, leaving me breathless, he whispered in my ear: "See you around."

He winked, jumped on the ship, and smiled playfully at me as they debarked. When I didn't hear from him again, I was not surprised. I figured I'd just fantasied the connection I'd felt, chalking it up to the so-called "Byron effect" which left women fainting in his path. But I should have realized, trusted my instincts, which told me that my chance meeting with Byron would completely redirect the course of my life.

The captain of the Aster didn't stir until the turbulent sea air jostled the small airship. It had been a smooth ride down the Italian coast, but as I guided the ship offshore, the sea breeze shook the gondola. Flying over water was always tricky. Flying over the water on a moonless night was even trickier. And I still hated flying over water. Suddenly, I was feeling exhausted.

The captain joined me at the wheel. "Any problems?" he asked with a yawn.

I shook my head. The skies had been dead. There had been no one and nothing else in the air. It was very late evening. I had been flying below the clouds so I could see the coastline rather than just trusting the ship's instruments. The cloud cover overhead was thick and black. There was not a star in the sky.

"I can take it from here," he said as he checked his instruments. "Just a couple more hours to go."

I nodded and went to the prow of the ship. I fished around in my satchel for my tobacco pipe. It was the last habit I allowed myself. I tried not to use it since it whet my already suffering appetite, but I carried it nonetheless. I lit the pipe, inhaled the stale tobacco, and watched the dark waves below. The taste filled my mouth, and soon I was imagining the tastes of all the other things I'd given up: the alcohol—absinthe in particular—opium, and Byron. In the end, I had given him up too, hadn't I?

It was not long before the dark shape of the Greek shoreline came into view. It rose out of the sea like a tomb. The *Aster* began to drop altitude. Again, I inhaled deeply. I let my mouth fill with the taste. As I exhaled, the smoke snaked from my mouth then dissipated in the wind.

CHAPTER 8

As we descended toward Missolonghi, my mind wandered to my first time racing the *Stargazer* on the international circuit. It was the New York City leg of the 1819 Grand Prix, and we didn't win. We placed second, but for our first entry internationally, we were happy. Cutter wasn't racing back then; the win had gone to the American racer, Bill Tallmadge, and his ship, the *Liberty*. Tallmadge, who died later that year in some street fight, was a hell of a drinker and a lot more fun than Cutter. Alejandro Ferdinand, the Spanish racer, had placed third. We were just coming off the winner's platform on the New York City towers, situated in Lower Manhattan, when a circle of tower guards escorted a small party from the notables' platform to greet us.

"Racers, your sponsors are here to congratulate you," the American Marshall had said.

While Tallmadge and Ferdinand moved forward without hesitation, Pidge, Angus, and I had all looked at one another. In 1819, you only needed a small fee to race in the British qualifying. We'd scrounged up enough running fares. The real problem was the entry fee for the World Grand Prix. All international racers had sponsors. We hadn't. Even though we'd won the British qualifying by "a fucking miracle," as Angus had called it, we didn't actually have the cash to race in the Prix. We'd flown to Amsterdam to work out a deal before the New York City leg. A stout, balding man in too-yellow pants had said: "*Stargazer?* But your sponsor already paid your fee."

"Who?" Angus had asked.

The man shook his head. "All I know is your account is settled," he'd said and handed us our papers.

Therefore, it gave us pause when we were told to meet our mysterious sponsor in New York. The American and Spanish teams stepped aside to reveal Lord Byron standing there, two well-shod gentlemen at his sides. I could not help but smile.

"I knew it," Pidge said in singsong under his breath. It had, in fact, been a running debate between the three of us over the identity of our sponsor. Pidge "knew" it was Byron. I'd always heard Byron lived perpetually in debt, his tastes grander than his bank account, so I'd had my doubts.

"Look who, in the end, caught who," Angus whispered in my ear.

Byron took me gently by the elbow, peeled off my sticky leather glove, and kissed the back of my hand. "Congratulations."

"Lord Byron, you have our thanks," Angus said.

Byron looked up at me from under his perfect eyebrows, his blue eyes flashing in the late afternoon sun. "Well, one can't just leave the fastest girl in England, and her team, without the means to race."

Angus smiled.

"My associates," Byron said then, introducing us to Percy Shelley and Edward Trelawny. I liked Edward right away, sensing he was exactly what he seemed, but Percy Shelley made my skin crawl: a hungry-eyed man. "Tonight, you will dine with me," Byron told me. "We've been invited by a notable New York family. I'll send a carriage. Where are you staying?"

"You can just send the carriage to the towers," I replied, hoping my cheeks had not reddened. I didn't want to tell him we'd planned to sleep on the ship.

"Very well," he said. "Well done, chaps," he added, clapping the boys on the shoulders, then walked off. As he walked away, I smiled. Perhaps that kiss, that feeling, had not been the "Byron effect" after all.

When the carriage arrived at the towers later that evening, Angus hurried me along. I'd become a mess of nerves. After all, what did I know about going to a formal dinner? It's not like Mr. Fletcher and Mr.

Oleander spent any time teaching me table etiquette. I suddenly felt miserable over how common I really was.

"But Angus," I groaned as I pulled up my long skirts and tried to get into the carriage, "I'm going to make a fool of myself, and worse, of him." I cursed as I stepped on the hem of the dress. My friend Celia, a dressmaker in London, had insisted I bring along something formal to wear just in case. She'd fashioned me something special. Modifying a traditional empire gown made of red satin, she'd sewn the union jack into the tail of the dress and cut the gown short in the front so I could sport an air jockey's traditional shorts or trousers and boots. "Beauty and function," she had said, but as I tried to load myself into the carriage, I cringed. I felt totally out of my element.

"Be yourself. He seems to like you as you are."

"But what about you and Pidge? I don't want to just leave you here."

"We're going to meet Tallmadge at Strawberry Hall. Come by when you're done."

I nodded.

"Stop worrying," Angus said, closing the carriage door behind me. He motioned to the driver. While Angus sounded confident, the lines around his mouth showed me that he was nervous for me. He waved as the carriage pulled away.

I sat in terrified silence as the carriage made its way down sparsely populated Fifth Avenue toward central

Manhattan. From the window, I saw massive mansions under construction all along the street. Otherwise, the place was an expansive wilderness. I must have taken a couple of doses of laudanum; by the time I arrived outside a pale-colored mansion, I was feeling remarkably light.

The driver helped me out. I was met at the door by a footman who asked me to wait in the foyer. Moments later, Byron arrived.

"How delightful," he said, taking me by the hand and giving me a spin so he could look over my gown.

"By the by, I don't even know where I am," I told him.

Byron grinned. "You're at the home of Katherine and Manson Mingott. Mingott has one foot in the grave so he's upstairs in bed, but Katy is keen on meeting you."

"Lord Byron, if you will, we are ready to seat you and your companion," a footman said.

Byron motioned affirmatively. "Are you ready?"

Definitely not. I nodded and put my hand in his.

Byron led me through a richly decorated parlor filled with fine furniture and expensive artwork toward the main dining room. Assembled in the parlor were at least a dozen other dinner guests who had to wait their turn to be seated after Byron—as custom dictated when there was a guest of honor. I took a deep breath.

"Who is that?" I heard one prim woman ask another from behind her dainty fan.

"That's the English airship racer," the second woman replied.

"Not her. Him!"

"Are you daft? That's Lord Byron."

"Lord Byron and Lily Stargazer," the footman announced.

I was puzzled. After dumping the name Fletcher, I had just been going by Lily. Why in the world had they married my name to my ship? My eyebrows furrowed. Had there been some confusion? I was about to say something to the footman when Byron laughed. I turned to look at him. "Wait, did you-"

"One can't go around without a surname. It's obscene, Miss Stargazer," he replied with a laugh.

After 1 moment, I laughed too. It was as good a name as any.

We were led into the dining hall where a long, ornate table had been set. Byron and I were greeted by the lady of the house, a toothsome and cheerful looking girl, about my age, whose breasts were larger than her head. "Lord Byron. Miss Stargazer. Welcome to my home. I'm Katy," she said with a wide smile.

"Madame, my thanks for your invitation," I said.

"Well, when I heard Lord Byron was in New York City, I was quick to invite him. It shall make for a rather good piece of gossip. I then learned the two of you are acquainted, so how could I resist?"

I wasn't quite sure how to reply, so when Byron laughed, I followed his lead.

The rest of the diners were seated shortly thereafter. I fretted as polite conversation began, tapping my fingers against my knee, wishing I'd smoked more opium before I'd left. Byron and I were introduced to the assembled company. I noticed that Byron remembered everyone's names at once. And he didn't fail to dazzle every woman in the room. They were glued to his face and every word. I couldn't blame them. His suit neatly tailored, a gardenia on his lapel, and his eyes sparkling in the glow of the crystal chandelier overhead, he was magnificent.

"I am told you are quite the race fan, Mrs. Mingott," Byron said to Katy as the footman served the soup.

"It's true! Miss Stargazer, I have to tell you, we picnicked on the roof of the mansion today to watch the race. We had a good view of your return from Philadelphia. For a moment, it almost looked like you would overtake Tallmadge," Katy said.

"Tallmadge knows the winds here better than I do. I was able to catch a wind shear and creep up on him, but in the end, he earned the win," I replied.

"How long have you been racing airships?" an elderly gentleman sitting across from me asked. Was his name Archer? I'd already forgotten.

"I was practically raised on an airship, Sir. My foster father owned transport ships. I barely remember a time when I wasn't on a ship, but I must have started piloting when I was about nine."

Intrigued, Byron raised an eyebrow at me.

"Are you the only female racer in the Prix?" a young woman sitting down the table from us asked. I wasn't sure from the look on her face if it was disdain or excitement she felt. Maybe she wasn't sure either.

"The Italians have a girl in the balloon basket, but I'm the only pilot."

"And the best in the British league! Quite a feat! We'll have our eyes on you for the rest of the Prix," Katy said cheerfully.

Despite Katy's pleasant demeanor, the dinner went on insufferably. First of all, everyone was drinking politely, which meant I wasn't drinking enough. And second, I had no idea how to negotiate proper table etiquette. Byron picked up on my confusion and discomfort. As inconspicuously as possible, he guided me through the meal. While the food was delicious, lobster bisque, platters of smoked salmon under heavy cream, braised venison in wine sauce, richly herbed mushrooms, and other divine dishes, I was glad when the main courses were done. I noticed that Byron savored the meal, complimenting the rich sauces and scrumptious plates.

"I'm so glad the food is to your taste," Katy had said.

"When food is prepared at its finest, it can bring great pleasure," he replied with a naughty wink that made Katy chuckle.

After the dessert, a light berry trifle, I was hoping we could leave. But then the conversation turned to poetry. All eyes in the room went to Byron.

"I do think poetry on the subject of love is the most divine," the same young woman down the table had just finished saying as she eyed Byron with such intensity that I had to grin.

Katy chuckled behind her hand.

Byron leaned back in his seat and put his hands behind his head. "The subject of love becomes boring. What I am interested in is passion," Byron replied.

"Is there a difference?" the girl asked.

"Of course," Byron said. He dropped one arm across my shoulders and stroked my neck with his fingers. Most of the women in the room look defeated. A chill traveled all the way to my toes. I turned and looked at him, his blue eyes meeting mine. "Passion is something rare. To feel passion is to feel something like love then something more. Love is commonplace. Love marries then grows weary. Passion burns."

"Yes, but passion burns out," Katy said.

"That's what makes the quest for passion so exhilarating," Byron replied excitedly. "What if you were able to find someone or something for which you felt unending passion?"

"As with writing poetry?" Katy asked.

Byron shrugged. "Poetry is craft. The passion fleets when the line is done. Lust and love are easy to come by, but unending passion . . . well, that is something I quest after. And is, no doubt, the key to my bad reputation."

Everyone laughed, including Byron.

"And you, Miss Stargazer, do you chase passion?" Katy asked me.

"Madame, you're more likely to find me chasing the green fairy," I replied, raising my aperitif toward her in toast.

Again, everyone chuckled.

"But what about racing?" she asked.

I smiled. "I don't think it's passion I feel when I fly. It's my natural element. I feel at home."

"Then are you in disagreement with Lord Byron about the quest for passion?" she asked slyly.

I looked at Byron. "Sometimes passion chases you." Under the table, I slid my hand up his leg and gently squeezed his thigh. My stomach trembled with excited butterflies.

Byron's eyes glimmered as he laughed out loud.

Everyone else at the table chuckled too. Soon, the diners began to depart. I was saying farewell to the others when Byron joined me.

"We are invited to an evening ball," he told me, motioning to Katy. "Shall we?"

Horrified, I suppressed a gasp. I had barely made it through the dinner without humiliating myself in front of the elegant crowd. "If you want to have some real fun, why don't you come with me instead?"

"Where?"

"Some of the racers are getting together at Strawberry Hall. There will be dancing, a different kind of dancing, there as well," I said with a grin.

Byron's eyes twinkled. "Would you dance for me there? You look stunning in this dress."

"You have to buy me a drink first."

"Then I'll give our regrets," he said with a grin.

Byron and I wished Katy farewell, thanking her for the invitation, then we left. I was relieved I had survived. Byron helped me into the carriage, but once the footman closed the door, we fell on one another in an almost a predatory way. His lips were hot and hungry. I wrapped my arms around his muscular frame and pulled him toward me, kissing him passionately. His sweet scent filled my senses. He held me by my waist and pressed his body against mine.

"I've been thinking about you for months," he whispered in my ear.

"I thought, well . . . I was too common for you," I admitted.

Byron pulled back and looked at me. "You are something rare," he said, kissing me gently on the lips. "I've never met anyone like you. You've an honest spirit. I live surrounded by people in masks."

"Then you need to choose better friends."

"Why do you think I followed you all the way to this god-forsaken place?"

I kissed him again, my tongue roving inside his mouth. I loved the taste of him. His mouth tasted sweet, like honey, the chemistry of his body melting with mine. I ran my fingers through his soft, curly hair. Pushing aside the collar on his silk shirt, I kissed his neck and shoulders. His bare skin was salty. We kissed until we reached the hall. When the carriage stopped, we were surprised.

"Come on," I said.

"Wait," Bryon replied as he looked me over. My hair, which had been nicely pulled up—well, as nicely as Angus could make it—hung in a rumpled mess. Byron pulled my hairpins out and shook my hair loose. With a satisfied nod, he then led me out of the carriage, passing a word to the driver before we headed toward the hall.

There was a loud cheer from the racers when we entered. "Lily!" Tallmadge screamed. His forehead was wet with sweat, and he half-rose, half-stumbled from his seat to welcome me. "Come on, come on, we've been waiting for you. Who is this strapping beast? Good lord, he looks like a gentleman."

"I'm George," Byron replied casually, shaking Tallmadge's extended hand. "Congratulations on your win."

"Christ, you English all sound so fucking grand. Thank you, George! Come have a drink. Lily, what's your poison?"

"Absinthe, if there is any to be found."

Tallmadge yelled to the bartender and led us to the corner where Tallmadge's team, friends, Angus and

Pidge, and a number of other racers had already gathered.

"My Lord!" Pidge yelled, raising his mug to Byron.

Byron smiled at him, and we pushed in beside Angus.

"Survived, did you?" Angus whispered to me.

"I guess."

"Looking a wee bit rumpled," he said with a laugh then shrugged. "You could do worse."

I punched him in the arm.

A tavern girl set down a dusty bottle of absinthe, a plate of sugar cubes, and a decanter of water in front of Byron and me.

"I don't know how you drink the stuff," Tallmadge yelled to us even though he was sitting close by. "It makes me see the fucking boogeyman."

"That's the pleasure of it," Byron said. "You never know where the green fairy will take you." He then prepared us both a glass.

"To passion," I said slyly, lifting my drink in toast.

"To passion," he replied, clicking his glass with mine.

In the corner, an Irish band was playing their fiddles furiously while a circle of dancing couples tried to keep pace. Byron pulled out a vial of laudanum, sharing with me, then we finished two drinks each. I noticed the others, who had been drinking far longer than we had, we already starting to drift into blissful forgetfulness.

"Now, let's see you dance," he said, taking my hand.

"Lily? Dance?" Pidge, who had been nursing the same mug of ale since we got there, said with a laugh. "Watch your toes, my Lord."

"I'm already a limping devil," Byron said with a laugh, tapping the heel of his bad foot. "What difference can it make?"

I smiled wryly at him, shook my head, then we took the floor. With a spin, Byron and I joined the other couples. They had just started a group dance. The racers started clapping and cheering us on.

I laughed loudly. "I admit it. I can't dance."

"Watch me, honey," a comely looking girl with spiraling blonde hair and wide blue eyes said. Then, very slowly, she showed me the steps. After a few embarrassing tries, I finally got it down.

My fingers lightly resting in Byron's hand, we soon began dancing, weaving between the others. Byron, so refined and sophisticated, looked a bit out of place amongst the rough crowd, but his cheerful enthusiasm brought him welcome. They probably didn't know who he was, but Byron had fun all the same—perhaps, because he had anonymity for once.

We were there for a couple of hours, mostly drinking and dancing a bit. When I noticed Byron's foot was paining him, I feigned tired. By then, most of the crowd had dispersed anyway. Angus and Pidge had left an hour before. Tallmadge was passed out in the corner with some half-dressed woman on his lap.

Byron and I were just getting ready to leave when I overheard a heated conversation between a couple standing near us.

"Let me go," a young woman told some bloke who had ahold of her wrist.

"I think not, girl. You've been looking for it all night," a drunk man twice her age replied.

The hairs on the back my neck rose as the ghosts of my past whispered from the grave.

The man yanked on the girl's arm. "You're coming with me."

"The hell I am," she replied and struggled to pull free.

He didn't let go.

"Let her go," I said, grabbing the man by the arm.

"Fuck off," he replied.

"I think not. She said let go."

"And why the fuck should I listen to some English tart? Fuck off, I told you," he said then shoved me.

I saw Byron make a move, but I was faster. Reeling back, I punched the man in the face. I heard something snap. The drunk yelped then clutched his jaw, letting go of the girl who made a break for it. The door banged closed behind her as she fled. Before Byron could intervene, the angry man swiped, catching me on the mouth. I felt the sting as my lip broke open followed by the taste of blood.

The bartender grabbed the drunk.

I grabbed Byron. "Let's just go," I said, pulling him toward the door. "It's not worth it."

"You fucking whore," the man yelled at me as he held his jaw.

Byron, who had reluctantly gone with me, turned. He pulled a knife from his boot as he crossed the room. He grabbed the man's hand and slammed it down on the bar. Raising his knife, he stabbed the drunk's hand, pinning it to the bar.

The drunk let out a scream.

"Never touch anything that's mine again," Byron said. He turned, pulled a handkerchief from his pocket, and handed it to me.

I blotted my lip as I got into the carriage. After that, the drink and the laudanum caught up with me. It all became a haze. I remembered riding across town in Byron's carriage, stopping outside an enormous mansion, and him carrying me though the hallways to his bedroom. He gently lay me down on his bed. I helped him pull off his shirt while he helped with the hooks on my dress. Soon we were both naked.

"Your lip," he said, gently touching the wound.

I pulled him into a passionate kiss. The pressure caused my lip to ache, but something about the marriage of the pain and pleasure made my heart beat quickly.

"Lily," he whispered aghast, pulling back. He touched his mouth where my blood stained his lips.

"It's all right," I said with a sigh.

Astonished, he smiled at me. He then kissed me all over my body. His touch was skilled, unlike mine. Despite growing up being over-exposed to sex, I was still inexperienced. I had been waiting, not for marriage, but for someone . . . special. Byron was certainly that. And at least my first time would be with someone who knew what they were doing. When Byron moved between my legs, I wanted to relax into it, but I felt momentarily shy.

"Haven't you . . . ?" he whispered.

I shook my head.

"I'll be gentle," he reassured me

But that wasn't what I wanted. I kissed him hard. "Don't be."

He looked inquisitively at me then our bodies moved together. The pain amplified the pleasure. Byron seemed hesitant at first, but seeing I enjoyed it, he did not hold back. Soon we were in the heat of it. I wanted to devour him. I bit him hard on the shoulders, tasting his sweat and flesh. He savored my aggressive embraces, pushing me to do more. His salty skin smelled divine. It went on like that for I don't know how long. More than once, we reached the pinnacle of pleasure. Finally exhausted, we fell into a tranquil bliss, Byron's arms wrapped around me.

"Passion," Byron whispered in my ear. "You bring me passion. You're so . . . natural . . . honest . . ."

"Not as much as I pretend," I said in a drowsy haze. It felt very important that he was not deceived about who I was. "My real name isn't even Lily. I'm just a worthless orphan from Cornwall. But I try," I sighed, "I try to do the right thing. To follow my instincts. To do right by everyone."

"Then you are the most honest person I've ever met," he replied, stroking my hair. "What is your real name?"

"Penelope," I replied without hesitation.

He kissed the back of my head. "Penelope," he whispered. The name sounded sweet on his tongue. "At least you found a way to fend off your demons. Mad Jack's lame son . . . I try to feed mine with anything, everything. Nothing satisfies. Nothing. It just burns. Sometimes I feel like it's consuming me."

"Then maybe you should try something different," I replied sleepily.

"Perhaps you're right," he said.

We fell into a deep sleep. When I woke the next morning, my head was pounding, and my lip ached. I opened my eyes to see the morning sunlight slanting in through the floor-to-ceiling windows. It cast its cheery glow on the ornate rug, which was decorated with embroidered dragonflies. I rolled over, expecting Byron would be gone, but found him sleeping beside me. As I was gazing at him, he woke groggily. He pulled me close, kissing my shoulder.

"Penelope," he whispered in my ear.

I closed my eyes. A tear streamed down my cheek. In my heart, I felt, all the while knowing that it was fleeting, passion.

CHAPTER 9

THE MORNING I ARRIVED IN Greece upon the *Aster*, the mist was rising slowly from the still waters around Missolonghi, a lagoon city in a swampy wetland. The entire place was draped in a pall of dreary gray. Not even the first rays of morning sunlight could penetrate the thick fog. The air was uncomfortably humid. My skin, though chilled with terror to goose bumps, felt sticky. Somewhere in the distance, loons called. Their voices echoed through the dismal, hollow space.

While there was an airship tower used by the military nearby, the captain piloted the <u>Aster</u> to the roof of the mansion where Byron was staying. He lowered the ship over the roof and dropped a ladder for the secretary and me to debark.

Even before we got down, Byron's Italian valet, Giovanni, met us on the roof.

Giovanni called to us. "Is that Lily?"

"It is," I yelled back.

Once I landed on the roof, I helped the secretary gain his footing. "Is he still alive?" I asked, turning to Giovanni.

He nodded sadly. "But worsening. You've made it just in time. The doctors have been arguing all night about what to do next."

"Come, Miss Stargazer, let's make haste," the secretary said, and we headed toward the stairs.

As I hurried across the roof, I heard a familiar sound call from overhead. It was the trumpet of a swan. I looked up. One swan flew over the building then disappeared into the mist.

"Lily?" Giovanni called.

I trembled.

We wound down the stairs into the mansion. Giovanni led us down marble hallways and through chamber after chamber. The place was utterly silent. I was surprised, then, when Giovanni opened the door to the last chamber to find the room filled with people.

"Vultures," Giovanni whispered under his breath.

It seemed like everyone who had ever been even remotely connected to Byron had assembled. Edward Trelawny, Mary Shelley, Tommy Moore, several Greek soldiers, and other of our friends were sitting in a small, closed alcove just off the salon. In the main chamber were relatives of Byron, cousins on his Gordon side, his half-sister Augusta-Leigh, Byron's ex-wife Annabella who still kept the title Lady Byron and her family members. When Giovanni had opened the door, everyone looked up.

"Oh no! Absolutely not!" Annabella said, aghast when she saw me. Outraged, she stood.

"I'll let him know you're here," Giovanni told me then crossed the room to enter the bedchamber.

They all began arguing with me, though I wasn't actually speaking to anyone, with the secretary, and with one another. I cast a glance toward Edward who nodded to me in acknowledgement.

"This is absurd! He won't see any of us. Not even his own family! Don't tell me that he is going to let *her* in," Augusta-Leigh shouted.

"That is for my Lord to determine," the secretary replied.

Annabella glared at me with such anger that it startled me. "He won't even see his own child, but he will see that opium eater? He must be out of his mind," she cursed.

The others started shouting, voicing their agreement with Lady Byron or arguing their own claims. They cursed about how Byron would only see Trelawny, his Greek slaves, or his other dogs, which I suppose included me, but not his proper family. Perhaps, I wanted to tell them, it was because Byron knew who was there for him and who was there for his estate. I was surprised, however, to hear he had not seen his daughter, Ada. I scanned the room. I had not seen her at first. Ada Byron, George's nine year old daughter, sat silently in the corner. Her eyes were glued to her hands, her bottom lip trembling.

The argument in the room grew very loud. People started pointing fingers in one another's faces. Edward and some of the others came into the salon and inserted themselves between the warring vultures. They were so loud that when Giovanni opened the door to motion me in, no one even noticed.

Quietly, I moved away from them. As I neared the door to the interior chamber, Ada Byron looked up at me. Her sad eyes were brimming with tears. And those eyes were just as clear, blue, and rich as her father's. Two large tears streamed down her cheeks.

"He won't see her?" I whispered to Giovanni.

"Lady Byron won't let Ada go without her. George will not see Lady Byron."

I gazed at the child who was staring at me. Behind me, a war raged on. Across from me, however, was a lonely little girl who was afraid she would never see her father alive again.

I held out my hand to her. "Come on," I whispered.

She cast a worried glance toward her mother who never looked back at her. She then took a deep breath, mustered up her courage, and came to me. She put her small hand in mine.

"He will be angry with you," Giovanni whispered to me.

I looked down at little Ada. Giovanni might be right. This one decision might cost me, but in Ada's eyes, I saw the reflection of myself standing at the door to the Charity School in Southwark. I wouldn't wish that experience on any child. "I know."

"There isn't one of us who hasn't thought of doing the same," Giovanni said then led Ada and me into the small antechamber between the rooms. "Wait here," Giovanni told us, disappearing into the bedchamber.

Ada drew a deep, shuddering breath. I knelt down to look her in the eyes. "What is it? Are you frightened?" I asked, pushing a strand of her dark hair behind her ear.

"Is my father a bad man?" she asked.

I was startled by her question. "A bad man?"

"My mother says he is wicked and that he will burn in hell. I should not like my father to burn in hell."

I considered her question. "Do you like horses?" I asked.

"Horses? Very much."

"Some horses are easy to ride. They take the saddle with no complaint and go gently for the rider. Some horses pull carriages and don't mind hard work. Other horses are wild. They run across the open fields with the wind in their manes and won't be captured. Your father is like one of those wild horses. He cannot live under a yoke. And when someone tries to tame him, he yearns to be free. But that doesn't make him wicked." I thought of the truly wicked men I'd known in my life. No, Byron was not wicked.

Ada sniffed, wiped her nose with her sleeve, and looked at me as she thought over my words. "Did you really leap from that airship in Paris?" she asked. "I saw the engraving in the newspaper. My mother called you Byron's fallen angel."

I laughed. "Yes, I did."

"Why?"

"Because if I had not jumped, someone I care for would have died."

"Weren't you afraid?"

"I didn't have time to be afraid."

"You just jumped . . . without thinking it over?"

"Sometimes the right thing to do is obvious."

Ada leaned her head against my chest. I put my arm around her and kissed the top of her head. After a moment, she pulled back and smiled at me. "Do you know what I heard?" she asked, placing her small hand on my chest above my heart.

I shook my head.

"A pegasus."

Giovanni opened the door. "He's ready for you," he said then added in a whisper, "I didn't tell him."

I took Ada's hand, squeezed it, then entered the darkened room.

The chamber had the stale smell of a sickroom. Medicines, sweat, incense, and other heavy smells choked the place. The curtains were drawn, the windows were closed. Inside, it was too warm and very still.

"Lily?" I heard Byron call weakly from the bed.

I could just make out his silhouette. He was sitting propped up by pillows, but his chin was on his chest, his head hanging.

"I'm here," I replied.

"Thank god," he more breathed than said. "Please come close."

"George . . . I . . . George, I've Ada here with me."

He was silent for a moment. "You brought Ada?"

"Yes."

"Annabella permitted it?" he asked weakly.

"No. I sneaked her in."

Byron laughed which caused him to cough heavily. "Come, my girls," he said finally.

I looked down at Ada who smiled up at me.

We crossed the room to Byron's beside. There, the once glorious man lay dying ingloriously. He was sickly pale, his skin tinted yellow around the eyes and lips. His face was swollen, his hair wet with sweat. A pungent, rotting smell effervesced from him. The sheen of fever made his eyes glimmer with sick madness while a strange shadow danced around the corners of his eyes. I had seen that shadow only once before; Mr. Fletcher's eyes had held that same shade as he'd lain dying on the street. I suppressed a shudder.

I helped Ada sit on the side of Byron's bed.

"I haven't seen you since you were a baby," Byron told Ada, reaching out to touch her cheek. "Do you remember me?" he asked her.

Ada did not answer right away. "No," she replied.

I realized that Ada had considered lying but had rejected the polite and political answer.

"I suppose your mother has taught you to fear me," Byron said with a sigh as he took his daughter's hand.

Ada lifted his hand and kissed it. "You are my father."

I smiled at the girl. No matter what Annabella had done to raise the child to hate him, the girl was Bryon's daughter through and through.

"I've read your poetry," Ada added. "I could never really believe that a bad man could create such beauty."

"My words are nothing compared to the daughter I created," Byron replied.

I choked back a sob. I dared not look at either of them.

The door to the bedchamber opened. "Pardon me, my Lord. Lady Byron has demanded that Ada return at once or that she be permitted to enter," Giovanni said.

With the door open, I could hear Lady Byron screaming at me. Having lost all sense of decorum in her fit of rage, Annabella was cursing me with words I was surprised she'd even heard before.

"Please, kiss your father once," Byron said to Ada, "before you go."

The child, who was now weeping, did as her father asked.

"Always remember that I loved you," I heard him whisper to her.

"I love you too," Ada said miserably then pulled away.

She crossed the room to Giovanni who waited for her with his arm outstretched. She looked back at her father once more before Giovanni closed the door behind them.

CHAPTER 10

"SHALL I OPEN THE CURTAINS? The sun is up," I said and went to the window.

He did not reply.

I pushed the curtains open. Weak sunlight shone in. The windows had a fabulous view over the gray waters of the lagoon. I cranked the window open a crack, hoping to let out the rancid smell. I took a deep breath and turned back. Byron sat with his head hanging low on his chest. His eyes were closed. Sitting gently, I took a spot on the bed beside him.

After a moment, he looked up at me. His eyes searched every shape and angle of my face. Without another word, he pulled me toward him and kissed me with urgent and frenzied passion. I was startled at first, and the woman I wanted to be, Sal's lover and companion, momentarily resisted. Byron frantically pulled me toward him, but he was weak. I felt his arms lose their strength. I gave in. I wrapped my arms around his thin, sickly frame. I let myself fall into him. All the love I had ever felt for him, denied feeling for him, and wanted to give to the man who could not be tamed rolled out of me like a storm cloud. Despite having let him go, I still felt intense passion for Byron. After several minutes, he fell back against the pillows in exhaustion.

"Oh my dear," I whispered, taking his hand in mine, stroking his cheek with the other. "How did this happen to you?"

"I was sick in the winter. The doctors insisted I should be bled. I never regained my strength," he said, his eyes closed. "Lily, water, please?"

I poured him a glass from the pitcher on the nightstand but didn't like the color of the liquid. I smelled it. It was stale. "Not this. You'll have fresh water," I said and rose.

I found Giovanni waiting in the antechamber. He rose when I opened the door. "Lily?"

"Bring a fresh pitcher of water. Can you search the kitchens for fresh mint? Wash it yourself and put it in the pitcher . . . and bring a fresh glass."

Giovanni nodded. "Of course."

I went back and sat once more beside Byron. I smiled softly at him.

"How did you know I wouldn't be angry with you for bringing Ada?" he asked.

"I didn't."

Byron kissed my hand. "There is no one in this world like you," he whispered then reached out and stroked my hair, his finger twisting around a ringlet in my locks.

I began to weep.

"Not yet," he said in a soft voice. He touched my chin, lifting my face toward him. I inhaled deeply, tried to catch my breath, and looked at him. His eyes were glued to my face.

"What are your doctors saying? Dr. Thomas?" I asked.

Byron started to cough. The deep coughs rattled through his chest. His whole body shook. I found a handkerchief on his side table; I handed it to him. He coughed hard into it. When he handed it back to me, I saw there was blood on the fabric. I became angry. Was this the best care they could give him? Why wasn't anyone doing anything?

"Dr. Thomas is not here yet. I called for him yesterday. I've two physicians in attendance: one wants to bleed me, the other thinks I need ammonia. I won't let them bleed me again."

Giovanni opened the door quietly, left the pitcher, then exited again.

I retrieved the minted water, which now smelled fresh, and poured Byron a glass. "Drink," I said. I guided Byron's hand to the glass and helped him lift it. He took just a few sips.

"My love . . . my passion," he whispered as I took the glass from him. He leaned back against the pillows and closed his eyes. He drifted back to sleep.

I scanned the room. On a table nearby the doctors had vials of medicines, odd and torturous looking medical equipment, and heaps of bandages. The room felt like a tomb. While he slept, I looked over Byron's bedclothes and blankets. They were stained with body fluids and soaked in sweat. Clearly, no one had cleaned him up in days.

I again went to the antechamber. "Giovanni, who the hell are the physicians attending him?"

"Dr. Bruno, he's new, and Mr. Millingen who was traveling with the army."

"Where is Dr. Thomas? The Englishman."

"In Zante. Lord Byron sent a messenger for him yesterday."

I frowned but held on to the hope that Dr. Thomas, who I knew well and liked, would arrive soon. "I need more fresh water, milled soap, lemons, and fresh linens. We need to get the room and Byron cleaned up. It's like a graveyard in there."

"Oh Lily, I wish he'd let us fetch you sooner."

"Why didn't he? Why are they here," I said, gesturing to the vultures outside, "but I'm the last to know?"

"He didn't want to interrupt your life. That was what he said."

I looked back at Byron, and in that moment, I hated everything about my life.

WHILE BYRON SLEPT, I SCRUBBED every surface of the room with soap and lemon. While the air outside was still unmoving, it was fresher than the air in the room. I covered him to his neck and opened all the windows. At my direction, Giovanni also had managed to scrounge up some springs of fresh lavender and jasmine. I filled Byron's room with vases of herbs. With Giovanni's and the secretary's help, we removed the soiled linens from Byron's bed while he slept. I sent heaps of stained and sweat-soaked linens away to be burnt. Byron woke only once and was disoriented.

"Mother?" he called weakly.

"It's all right, George," I said. "We're just putting on fresh linens."

"My foot is hurting again," he said in a small, feeble voice.

I moved toward his malformed foot, but the secretary reached out to stop me.

"He would never permit it," he whispered aghast.

I shook his hand off and removed the stocking covering Byron's foot. The clubbed foot, which often pained him, looked far more swollen than usual.

"Heat a towel," I whispered to Giovanni.

The secretary frowned disapprovingly and left in a huff.

Giovanni returned a few minutes later with a hot, damp towel.

"I can take it from here," I said.

Giovanni nodded and went back into the antechamber.

Gently, I applied the warm cloth to Byron's foot.

"It aches," Byron groaned.

"The heat will comfort it," I told him.

Byron seemed surprised to hear my voice. He opened his eyes wide. "Lily!" he said aghast and tried to pull his foot away.

"Stop that. Let me finish," I said, and gripping him firmly, I wrapped the heated towel around his foot.

I saw a war rage behind his eyes. He wanted to be angry, but in the end, he softened. "It smells like lemons in here."

"I hope so. Everything in the room is clean now . . . besides you."

My normally prim poet still looked and smelled like a walking corpse. "Will you help me?" he asked quietly.

"Of course."

I finished caring for Byron's foot then went to his dresser to pull out a clean bedgown. On the top of his bureau, Byron had a small bottle of cologne. I opened it and inhaled deeply. The sweet scent of orange blossom and patchouli filled my senses. This was the

Byron I knew. I prepared a basin with soapy water, sprinkled in some cologne, and set it beside his bed. I closed the windows and came to his bedside.

"Okay, let's get you out of this," I said as I helped him sit up. He was so weak. I began to fear that redressing him might be too much for him. Gently, I pulled the clothes off him, keeping him covered all the while. Carefully, I took one limb at a time out from under the fresh blankets and washed what looked like a month's worth of grime from his skin.

"Do you remember New York? You bathed me then too . . . the morning after . . . of course, we were both in the tub," he said with a naughty smile, a glimmer of his true self shining through.

"Remember? What kind of woman forgets her first time?"

"Not your kind."

Outside, a spring rain started to fall. Thunder rolled across the misty horizon. I stroked the wet towel across his chest. He had lost much of his muscle tone, his chest and stomach now soft. I washed him gently. Seeing him in such a state filled my heart with terror. I set the wet cloth aside, dried him, then gently redressed him in fresh clothes.

"Angus . . . he wanted me to-" I began, but Byron put a finger to my lips.

"Has the tinker married you yet?" he whispered.

"No."

"He'll ask," Byron said as he gently stroked my hair. He then dropped his hand and closed his eyes. He became very still and silent.

I put my hand on his forehead. His fever burned. "George?"

"Lily . . ."

"Drink some cool water," I said, lifting the glass to his lips.

Weakly, he took a sip. "I wanted to marry you," he said, his voice sounding hollow, "but feared what I might do to you . . . to us. Despite all my rough ways, all my life I wanted to be a married man. I loved the vision of it, but my time with a 'suitable match' like Annabella taught me I was no good for anyone. Certainly, no good for someone I actually love."

"I liked us as we were."

"But in the end, it wasn't enough, was it? I am awash with regrets . . . more than I can name . . . so many more than I can name," he whispered tiredly then fell asleep, leaving me to weep in private.

CHAPTER 11

AN HOUR LATER, BRYON'S DOCTORS entered the room in the middle of a flustered argument. The elder of the two was speaking scornfully to the younger man. Giovanni and the secretary trailed miserably behind them.

"What is this?" the elder, dressed in dark robes like an undertaker, demanded as he eyed the room over.

"A clean and proper sick room," I replied, standing. Byron still slept soundly.

"Who are you?" the second, younger doctor asked me.

"Who are *you?*" I replied.

"Julius Millingen. I am the army surgeon."

After my run-in with Julius Grant, I decided it was not my week for dealing with men named Julius. "Lily Stargazer."

"Well, I'll be!" Mr. Millingen replied, astounded.

"Madame, I'm Dr. Bruno," the elder doctor said. "We need to examine Lord Byron. Please step out."

"Dr. Bruno, begging your pardon, but unless you plan on putting a pistol to my head, I'm not going anywhere."

Dr. Bruno exhaled in exasperation. "I've no time for the romantic ideas of one of Lord Byron's girls. Please remove this wo-" he was saying to Giovanni when I crossed the room and grabbed the good doctor by the throat, cutting him off mid-sentence.

"Not another word," I said. "I don't know who you think I am, but I'm not moving an inch because as far as I can see, you must have learned medicine in a gutter," I said then let him go.

"Clearly, Madame," Dr. Bruno said, rubbing his throat, "you are an expert on gutters."

"That's enough, Francesco," Byron roared from his bed in a rare moment of strength.

"Lord Byron, do forgive me. Certainly, there is no problem if you wish her presence," Dr. Bruno said, glaring at me. "We've come to check your condition."

Byron motioned for him to proceed.

I stood with Giovanni and the secretary at the end of Byron's bed and watched as they worked him over. They examined his mouth and eyes, listened to his breath, his heart, and prodded his body far more roughly than I was comfortable watching.

"Is this the doctor who bled him?" I whispered to Giovanni.

He nodded. "Yes, sour old apple."

"Are there no better doctors to be found?"

"We are waiting for Dr. Thomas."

I frowned.

"My Lord, I am still seeing signs of inflammation. You must consider bloodletting. I assure you, it will let the poison from your body and ease the inflammation. It will save your life," Dr. Bruno said.

Byron shook his head. "No. What say you, Mr. Millingen?"

"My Lord, I believe the bloodletting can wait, but I do suggest we try ammonia to help the condition."

"Which is ridiculous," Dr. Bruno replied. "The longer you hold off the bloodletting, the worse the condition will become."

Byron closed his eyes. "Dr. Bruno, I am beginning to think you want to grow famous by saving me through the bloodletting. The same treatment, proscribed again by you, nearly killed me this winter. I'll not permit it . . . nor the ammonia for now. Giovanni, where is Dr. Thomas? I sent for him more than a week ago!"

Raising an eyebrow, I looked at Giovanni.

"En route, my Lord."

"I'm beginning to think he is delaying on purpose. And where is Lily? I have been calling for her! Hasn't she come yet?"

"I'm here, George."

He opened his eyes and looked at me. "Yes," he said then, seeming to realize his confusion. "Yes, that's right." Byron then eyed over the doctors. He sighed. "Both of you, get out. Giovanni, go find a witch in the village. I'm better off with a toothless soothsayer than these learned doctors."

"My Lord," Dr. Bruno said bitterly as he bowed then exited.

"My Lord," Mr. Millingen echoed, following behind Dr. Bruno.

I grabbed Giovanni as he headed toward the door. "We need to fetch the nearest local doctors, as many minds as can be gathered today. Send Edward and tell him it's urgent. These men know nothing. We need other learned opinions and quickly."

Giovanni nodded and went back out.

I turned then to the secretary. "Please, have some broth and fresh bread sent up."

The secretary nodded.

"Lily?" Byron called.

"I'm here," I said, closing the door behind them. I went back to Byron's bedside.

"I think they are trying to kill me."

"They are struggling to know the best course of treatment. Your condition seems to be worsening."

"I'm so tired," he said and reached out to take my hand, falling asleep immediately thereafter.

A short while later, I heard commotion in the courtyard. I went to the window and looked out to see Edward and several military men mustering. There were at least a dozen riders. Edward was shouting orders. He gazed up at me. I waved to him. He waved back to me then spurred his horse out the gate. The other riders followed behind him, all setting off in different directions when they reached the road. I closed my eyes and prayed for good fortune, because when I looked back at Byron again, I could swear I saw the shadows drawing closer.

CHAPTER 12

THE SECRETARY RETURNED WITH BROTH and bread. I broke some pieces into the liquid. "George, please wake up and eat something," I said, kissing him gently on the cheek.

"What is it?" he asked tiredly.

"Food. You need to try to eat something."

Byron opened his eyes sleepily. He looked over the meager offerings.

"I know, not quite in line with your normal tastes. No butter or cream or wine. But it is something," I said, tapping the spoon on the side of the bowl.

He tried to smile at my joke. He adjusted himself as best he could, and to my surprise, he let me feed him. He was quiet, which was very unlike him. As if swallowing pained him, he ate very slowly. After he got down just a few spoonfuls, he motioned for me to put the food aside.

I poured him another glass of water and lifted the cup to his lips. The liquid spilled from the corner of his mouth. I wiped off the water and tried to keep up a brave face. My façade, however, was beginning to crack. And so was Byron's.

"Set it aside," he whispered. "Come lie by me."

I pulled off my boots and climbed into the bed with him.

"Is it cold?" he asked.

"No," I said then felt him for fever. He was burning.

"Is it day or night?"

"Night."

"Is Edward here?"

"Yes, but I sent him on an errand."

"An errand?"

"Yes."

"Will he be back soon?"

"Yes."

"Where did you send him?"

"To fetch another doctor."

"Why?"

"Because I don't like Dr. Bruno, and Mr. Millingen strikes me as an idiot."

"Is Dr. Thomas here yet?"

"No."

He was silent for a while. "It took so long for you to come."

"Why didn't you send for me earlier?"

He was silent again, but after several minutes, he whispered my name. "Lily," he said, gently cradling my face against his. Face to face, I felt the hot tears on his cheeks. "Lily . . ." he whispered again then broke into a sob. "Penelope . . . I love you so much. I am so sorry I let you go. I am so sorry . . . I did it for you . . . but I regretted . . . I never should have let you go. You were always my passion. I've never loved anyone as I've loved you."

"I love you too," I whispered, my heart breaking. "Still. And always."

He kissed my face over and over again. His skin burned against my cheek, the salty taste of his tears wet my lips. I would never be able to forgive myself. The magic of Aphrodite had blinded me. I had given up my soul's mate. I had talked myself into a simple life I was not even sure I wanted over the deeper, mysterious connection George and I shared, and I hated myself for it.

"When I am gone, they will say wicked things about me. I could never shake the pagan inside me. But it was different with you," he rasped into my ear.

"You can still recover. You must be strong."

"I'm too far gone," he whispered. "Keep me in your heart. I will journey there with you."

"No," I groaned. My chest ached desperately. "No, don't talk like that."

"Penelope," he whispered, clutching my face. "Never leave me again."

"No. Never again."

His cheek pressed against mine, Byron exhaled deeply then slept again. Lost to misery, I lay weeping desperately.

SOMETIME AFTER MIDNIGHT, I WOKE to hear Byron muttering.

"What is it? Do you need something?" I asked.

"Tell me again," he whispered.

"George?"

"Tell me again about Gight."

Gight Castle, his ancestral birthright, had been sold in the months before his birth to pay off Mad Jack's, Byron's father's, gambling debts. Byron had never lived in the castle. Instead, he'd spent his youth living in near poverty, abandoned by his father. The castle had passed to his vulture cousins who were sitting in the salon outside. It was a loss, a near miss, which had always haunted him.

"Tell me," he whispered. I was certain that it was not me he was seeing, it was his mother.

"It is a beautiful castle sitting in the middle of a green field . . .," I began, lying as best I could, tears streaming down my face. I had never seen Gight

Castle, but by the time I finished weaving my tale, he'd already fallen back to sleep.

Sometime later, Mr. Millingen came in and examined Byron. He shook his head. "We need to do something soon," he whispered then left.

Deep in the night, Byron woke in a fit of anger: "Why would you tell such sick lies about me? About me and my own sister! What is wrong with you?" he screamed in my face, a look of such raw hatred in his expression that I shrank from him.

"George, it's Lily," I said quietly. "I'm Lily." It was Annabella he was seeing.

"Lily?" He squinted away his confusion. "Lily . . . why did you leave me for that tinker?" he spat then fell back to sleep.

I buried my head against his chest and wept. I didn't know the answer to that question anymore.

I must have dozed off then, because sometime after, Edward quietly entered the chamber.

"Lily?" he whispered.

I wiped my eyes and sat up. The room was dark save the candle Edward carried. "Light the lamps," I replied.

"He's sleeping?"

"Fitfully. He was asking about you earlier. I told him you'd be back soon."

"Christ, what a disaster. We managed to bring in three local doctors. They are in a room below arguing with one another."

"Is there a consensus?"

"Millingen has nearly convinced them Byron has become languid. They want to give him ammonia."

"And Dr. Bruno?"

"He said that if the ammonia is administered, he will leave."

"Do we know when we can expect Dr. Thomas?"

"A transport arrived tonight saying the doctor will depart Zante at earliest tomorrow evening. His wife is in childbirth."

It would be too late. "What do we do?"

Edward shook his head. "What choice do we have?"

I looked back at Byron. In the long shadows cast by the lamp lights, he already looked like a corpse.

"He won't make it. We have to let them try something," Edward said. "Is he still lucid?"

"I'm not sure."

"We need to wake him. It needs to be his decision."

"All right."

"I'll bring the doctors."

"All right."

"I'm glad you came, Stargazer," Edward whispered. "He needed you."

I took a deep breath and went back to the bedside. "George?" I called, kissing his hand. "George, can you wake?"

He opened his eyes groggily. "Yes."

"Edward is going to bring in some doctors to speak with you," I told him.

He motioned toward the pitcher of water on the table.

I poured him a glass and helped him drink.

"Is Dr. Thomas here?" he asked.

"No. His wife is in childbirth. He is delayed."

Byron looked distressed. "Perhaps they will name the child after me in memorial," he laughed ruefully.

"Don't say things like that!"

Byron reached out and touched my cheek. "Do you think I will get well?"

"Yes."

"Then let's make it a match," he said.

"A match?"

"If I live-"

"You will live."

"If I live . . . you will marry me." He stared at me with heartbreaking intensity.

For a moment, guilty misgivings bubbled up regarding Sal, but I brushed them away with panicked haste. "It won't kill our passion?"

"Nothing can kill our passion."

"Then, agreed."

Byron smiled. "Go to my bureau," he instructed. "From the top drawer, bring the box with the pocket watch."

I was puzzled, but I did as he asked. I rooted through the drawer until I found the box. Inside was an ornate pocket watch. I sat beside him and handed him the box. He removed the watch and tossed it aside. He then pulled off the velvet lining to reveal two items which had been hidden; he handed them to me. One item was an ancient looking key, and the other was a slim piece of copper punched with square holes.

"And if I die, you will take these keys to the Bank of Scotland in Edinburgh and ask for the bank president. Refuse to see anyone else. Tell him you are there with the key to my vault."

"Your vault?"

"You must never let these keys leave your sight. No matter what happens, you must be the one who takes the keys to the bank. It is imperative that it is you who opens the vault and no other."

"What's in the vault?"

"You will only learn that if I die. Otherwise, I'll tell you after the wedding."

"George."

"Lily," he said, grabbing my wrist tightly, "it is desperately important that you are the one to open the vault. Do you understand me?"

"Yes."

"Are you certain?"

"Yes."

"Don't delay. Be sure you see to it no matter what," he said then let me go. My wrist ached.

"I promise," I said, slipping the keys into my bodice.

Byron seemed satisfied that I had understood. He rubbed his temples.

"Can I get you something?" I asked.

Byron sighed heavily. "Tea?"

I went to the fire and banked it up, setting the teapot on to heat. As I was preparing the tea, I heard a knock on the door. Giovanni entered. "Lily? My Lord? Edward is here with the doctors."

"Send Edward in alone," Byron replied.

I busied myself with the tea while Edward and Byron talked. As he had done with me, Byron instructed Edward to take a package from his belongings.

"My remaining poems. Send them to my publisher," he told Edward who had murmured in assent. "And my personal journals. Do with them what you will." I turned to look. Edward was holding a large bag that contained several leather-bound journals. Byron saw me looking at the bag. "Don't worry. Our world is private," he told me.

Edward looked back at me. His anguished expression frightened me.

"Your tea is ready," was all I could stammer out.

"At least I will die like a Baron," Byron said with a laugh.

The china rattled in my hands as I crossed the room.

"She'll throw herself from an airship but is afraid to see me sick. You're making me nervous, Lily," Byron said.

Carefully, I lifted the teacup to his mouth and helped him take a drink.

Ahh," he sighed after taking a sip. "You always knew just how much to sweeten it," he added then turned to Edward. "Well, let's hear what the leeches advise." With that, Edward motioned for Giovanni to let the doctors inside.

I sat at Byron's beside, holding his hand. Fear had frozen my heart. I prayed they would not bleed him.

Mr. Millingen spoke the most. " . . . and we believe that you are no longer suffering from inflammation but are languid due to the long lung complaints. We are of the opinion that carbonate of ammonia will rid you of the lingering aliment."

"What say you, Dr. Bruno?" Byron asked.

"If you agree to it, my Lord, I will leave this night. I will not have your death on my head."

"But you still urge the bleeding?"

"Yes, and a copious amount," Dr. Bruno replied.

Byron looked thoughtful. I worried about his ability to make a clear decision given his mental and physical state. "The rest of you . . . are you all in agreement?" he asked the others.

They nodded. I remained frozen.

"They . . . we . . . are," Mr. Millingen said.

"Then prepare the treatment."

"You'll kill him!" Dr. Bruno shouted, storming from the room. His certainty terrified me.

I looked at Byron. His head bobbed drowsily. I touched his forehead. Fever ravaged him. When he looked up at me, he looked frightened.

"Edward?" Byron called.

"I'm here."

Byron nodded.

After a few moments, Mr. Millingen brought Byron a tonic.

Byron took the vial and lifted it to his mouth. He paused for a single moment and looked at me. "My passion," he whispered.

I felt like a hand had gripped my throat. I squeezed his fingers. "And mine," I whispered.

He drank, grimacing at the taste.

"I'll get you some water," I said and rose. The doctors had moved the water pitcher to the medical prep table. As I was pouring a glass, I heard a strange sound behind me. Byron took a sharp, wheezing breath. I turned in time to see him start convulsing.

"He's seizing," Mr. Millingen yelled. "Hold him down! Hold him down!"

The doctors rushed to Byron's bedside.

The glass I was holding slipped from my hand and fell to the floor with a crash.

"Get the opium distillation. We need to calm him," Mr. Millingen shouted to the other doctors.

They forced Byron's mouth open and poured the opium concoction down his throat. I was horrified to see it splash all over his face and clothes as he thrashed violently. After a few moments, he went still.

"What the fuck was that?!" Edward screamed at Mr. Millingen. "Is he dead?"

The doctor took out his wooden stethoscope and listened to Byron's heart.

"Is he dead?" Edward yelled again.

I couldn't breathe.

"Shut up," Mr. Millingen spat. "Everyone be quiet."

We all waited. "Lord Byron?" Mr. Millingen called. "Give me the salts," he said motioning to another doctor who brought a vial of strong smelling salts. "Lord Byron?" Mr. Millingen called again, waving the vial under Byron's nose.

Byron lay pale and still on the bed, his body twisted at a strange angle.

"He's alive, but in a deep sleep," Mr. Millingen pronounced. He shook his head. "He won't wake again."

Infuriated, Edward and I cleared the doctors out, allowing only Dr. Millingen to remain in the antechamber outside. I cleaned Byron up and arranged his body comfortably on the bed.

"Someone should tell the vultures," I said.

Edward exchanged words with the secretary who went to inform the family of Byron's condition. I crawled back into the bed with Byron. I lay my head on his chest. His heart was still beating but very slowly.

Edward took a seat near the bed, folded his hands across his chest, and rested his chin on his knuckles. Giovanni sat weeping nearby. From the salon outside, I heard crying.

I lifted Byron's still-warm fingers and kissed them. "Don't forget our match," I whispered in his ear. "Wake up, George. Wake up and marry me. We don't have to be apart again," I said and gently kissed him. I closed my eyes and wept, my head pressed against his chest. I was still lying like that when, an hour later, his heart stopped beating. My passion was gone. And everything I thought I knew about who I was no longer mattered.

CHAPTER 13

I HEARD THE INHUMAN WAIL that came out of my mouth with detachment. I felt like I was watching the scene from outside of my body. Edward was trying to pull me from Byron while Dr. Millingen rushed to save him. There was nothing to be done.

I heard myself screaming a succession of "No! No! No! No!" as Edward then Giovanni pulled me away. "George!" I screamed at Byron who did not move. "George!" I yelled, trashing against Giovanni who would not let me go. Finally pulling me to the ground, he held me tightly as I wept with such howling desperation that, in the end, I blacked out.

I woke moments later to Giovanni carrying me out of the room. "You need to come away now," he said tearfully. "It's over." I looked back at Byron. A pale, sickly corpse lay in his place. Giovanni took me to a private room nearby. "Rest, Lily. Rest now," he said, lowering me onto a bed. He drew the curtains then left me alone to my grief. I wept and wept until I felt entirely empty. My head throbbed. I cursed myself to the depths of my being, hating myself for what I had given up. Weeping hysterically, I dropped into a tormented oblivion, aching with bottomless pain.

A few hours later, I woke with swollen eyes, a pounding head, and a sick feeling of emptiness inside me. A crack in the curtains let in the first morning light. It was just after dawn. I crawled out of bed and headed back to the salon. I'd left my boots in Byron's room. Barefoot, I padded down the cold marble hallway. The salon was now empty save the small alcove where Edward, Giovanni, Mary, Tommy, several soldiers, and other good friends were sitting around a large round table. Empty bottles littered the tabletop. They were all laughing loudly and talking about Byron. The room was full of smoke: tobacco and opium. They were just pouring another round of drinks when I arrived. I pulled up a chair beside Edward. He slid an empty glass toward me. I slid it back then plucked a bottle of gin from the center of the table. I pulled the cork out with my teeth.

"To Byron," I said and hoisted the bottle.

"Here, here," they all cheered.

"Wait," Mary called, stopping us. "Give a proper toast," she said as she looked around the table.

"Everyone, use your right hand. That is how you toast properly."

"No, no," Tommy corrected. "Not this time. My ma always said, on the other side, in the spirit world, they see us in opposite. Everyone, use your left hand. He will see it as our right."

Mary nodded then switched her glass to the opposite hand. "Then to Byron," she called.

"To Byron," I whispered, toasting him with my left hand. I drank the liquor like it was water. The sweet taste of alcohol filled my body. Having gone so long without a drink, the alcohol hit me hard. It was what I wanted. Sweet nothingness. When someone pulled out an opium pipe, I was more than grateful.

"Don't let Stargazer get it. You'll never get it back," Edward joked.

He was right. I smoked it all, convincing myself not to feel bad about it. Everyone understood. Mary Shelley, who I liked much better than her late husband Percy, filled the pipe again and pushed it toward me.

Edward then told the tale of the first time he ever saw me: "Byron suddenly got it into his mind that he wanted to watch the 1819 British airship qualifying, of all the bloody things, which baffled the hell out of Percy and me," he began. "Byron wasn't one to really give a damn about cheap sporting events, no offense, Lily, but days before the race, he had us all scurrying about getting ready to go. Mind you, we had to fly to London to watch the event."

"Byron hauled you back to Britain? But I thought he'd swore he'd never return from exile," Mary said.

"That was what we said, but he insisted. Next thing we knew, we were floating over the Thames watching the racers come in. Percy and I were debating how much coin Byron had riding on the winner—which was the only reason we could come up with on why he'd come—when Byron got very excited. He ran to the prow of the ship with a spyglass and hung off the ship to watch."

"'Take a look,'" Percy had said to me as he looked on. "'Now I see what all the fuss is about.'"

"I picked up a lens and caught sight of our illustrious airship racer for the first time," Edward said, patting my shoulder. "Lily was bouncing all over the deck, tugging lines and yelling at her crew, as her ship pulled into first. By god, Byron was smiling from ear to ear."

"Percy asked, 'Who is she?' Byron never answered him, he only smiled and watched you pilot in. When they signaled you'd won first place, Byron screamed aloud for you. Christ, I don't think I ever saw him look so . . . happy."

"'New girl,'" I remember saying, "'Who is she?' I'd asked him. Byron never answered. He only motioned to the captain that he was ready to go. That's when I knew, that girl had to be someone special. I always wondered what you'd done to get under his skin like that."

I sat weeping. "Nothing," I whispered.

Someone managed to dredge me up a bottle of absinthe. Determined to squelch my spirit somewhere beyond feeling, I poured myself glass after glass. Part of me hoped the green fairy would lead me to the otherworld and just leave me there. The room soon became a distorted mess of color, sound, and people who were crying, shouting, or laughing loudly.

They told story after story of Byron's exploits the world over, some of which surprised even me. I had not known that he'd been rumored to be the lover of Albanian overlord Ali Pasha during his first youthful exploits abroad. The thought of it had me laughing.

At some point late in the day, I'd gotten up and tried to see Byron, but his secretary refused me.

"I'm sorry, Miss Stargazer. This time is set aside for family viewing only," he said.

His answer confused me. Family viewing? The man lying dead inside should have been my husband. Enraged, I took a swipe at the man.

Edward, who had been by my side, stopped me. "No you don't, Lily. Don't worry. There will be time for his real family and his *loyal* friends later," Edward said, glaring at the secretary as he guided me back to the alcove.

But after a while, I noticed Byron's room was no longer guarded. I sneaked in. I wanted so desperately to be near him one last time. They had laid him out so that he was fit for viewing by his family and political acquaintances. He was dressed in a clean, white, Greek-fashioned toga. They had even crowned him with a wreath of laurel. He was so . . . still.

Passing his corpse, I staggered to Byron's bureau. Though it took me five tries to finally catch the drawer pull, I opened his dresser and pulled out one of his white dress shirts. I buried my face in it, soaking up his smell. I then stole the bottle of cologne from the top of his dresser.

I turned again to look at him. His white skin seemed luminescent in my opium and absinthe haze. Then, to my shocked amazement, I spotted his shade standing beside his body. I felt a strange double vision, seeing the dead man and his spirit all at once. The ethereal, opalescent creature standing over the corpse looked at me with wild, twinkling blue eyes. "Penelope of Arcadia," he said, grinning madly. "My true passion! For you and through you my regrets will be mended!" he laughed then spun dizzily, disappearing back into the ether.

I closed my eyes hard, trying to shake off the hallucination. When I opened them again, the vision had gone. My boots and satchel were sitting forgotten near the head of the bed. I bent and stuck his shirt and cologne into my bag, strapping the satchel across my body. As I did so, I eyed his corpse more closely. How still he was. I knew it was better if I didn't, but I wanted to touch him just one more time. I set my fingertips on his lips. They were ghastly cold. It startled me so horribly that I screamed.

Out of nowhere, Edward came and pulled me away. "Come on, Lily. Let's get out of this place," he said, holding me. "My Lord, if you don't mind, I think I'll take your girl away from all this misery," he told the corpse and led me by the hand down the hallways of the mansion.

I stumbled along weeping miserably. I was so intoxicated that I started to lose time. In what felt like a minute later, I was on horseback. The next minute, I was sitting on the deck of an airship. A man I did not know was injecting my arm with morphine. I smiled blissfully. When I opened my eyes again, I found an opium pipe, almost fully smoked, resting in my hands. Several people on the deck of the airship were dancing and drinking wildly. I lifted the pipe and smoked again. I leaned back on the deck of the ship and gazed up at the sky. It was early evening. In the dim twilight, one exceptionally brilliant star shone in western sky.

"Go to hell!" I screamed at the sky. "Go to hell!"

Around me, everyone laughed.

I threw the pipe overboard and drifted into unconsciousness.

CHAPTER 14

THE BRIGHT MORNING LIGHT HURT my eyes so terribly I could barely open them. A beautiful yet haunting chant echoed through my room from somewhere nearby. Slowly, I opened my eyes to find myself lying in a large bed; the curved wood design of the frame, the orange and purple beaded curtains, and crimson-colored silk sheets came slowly into focus. Otherwise, the room was all white: white marble floors, white marble walls, white marble ceiling. The evocative, reverberating sound was coming from outside my window. The ornate shutters on the windows were open. I spotted the tall spire of a nearby mosque. Beyond the spire were airship towers I did not recognize.

I closed my eyes again and listened. The beautiful yet melancholy noise made my heart ache. My very soul felt pained. I rolled over and gazed at the rays of sunlight slanting in through the open window. I reached out to touch the motes of dust floating in the air. I wanted to die.

I then spotted my satchel sitting beside the bed. Dangling my hand over, I opened the bag and pulled out his shirt. I crushed it to my face, inhaling deeply. Things would never be the same again.

I lay back and looked at the canopy. Overhead, multicolored glass lanterns stirred, their chains chiming in the soft breeze. Suddenly remembering, I grabbed at my chest. I was still wearing my bodice, and the keys were still safely hidden within. I pulled them out. The heavy metal key looked very old. The small copper piece, which Byron called a key, looked like nothing of the sort. It was long, slim, and was punched with square holes. I held it up and looked through the holes out the window, the metal making a kind of unnatural cobweb. I clutched it against my chest.

"Ah, Madame, you are awake," I heard someone say. I turned to find a woman standing in the doorway. Her body, save her eyes, was entirely covered in veils.

"Where am I?" I rasped, my throat parched.

"Morocco."

While I didn't remember how I'd come there, or how long I'd been there, the taste in my mouth, the injection marks down my arms, and the burning ache in my body told the tale. "The man I was with-"

"Mr. Trelawny is still asleep down the hall."

I sat up. I was dressed only in my bodice and underwear, but, thankfully, I'd woken up alone. "I need to leave," I told her.

"You do know, Madame, you are on the Barbary."

I understood where I was even if I didn't remember how I'd gotten there. I was in the heart of pirate country. I held my head. It ached miserably. "There is always a transport for hire."

The woman nodded affirmatively and helped me get up. I was suddenly overwhelmed with vertigo. I caught a glimpse of myself in the mirror: my cheeks were hollow, skin pale, eyes bloodshot and dark ringed. My hair hung in a tattered mess all around my face. "How long have I been here?"

"I'm not certain . . . perhaps a week?"

A week? I squinted my eyes shut and tried to remember. My memory was a confused jumble of distorted images. I tried to dredge up some memories of what had happened, where I had been, but when I did, images of Byron's cold corpse insisted themselves upon me. I opened my eyes, thrusting the heartbreaking images away.

"Perhaps I can bring you something clean to wear?" the woman said, lifting the clothes I'd been wearing since I'd left London. The smell of opium, alcohol, and body odor reeked from them.

I scanned the room. Save my satchel, I had nothing with me. And my feet were still bare. My boots had been left by Byron's bedside. I envisioned them sitting like silent, unseen watchmen standing vigil over his body. My head pounded; I started to feel nauseous. I was glad to see there was a vial of laudanum sitting on my bed table. "Please . . . and I need shoes, if you can find some."

The woman said nothing but exited the room.

I sat back down on the bed and took a drop of laudanum. All that mattered was that it dulled the ache. I rubbed the injection marks on my arms. They itched terribly. An image flashed through my mind of a robed man with rotten teeth and a deafening laugh injecting me with a sharpened quill attached to a rude bladder full of morphine. My stomach quaked as I held back bile. Curling back up on the bed, I clutched Byron's shirt. I recalled the softness of his hair against my cheek and the feel of his hot breath whispering in my ear. Memories flooded my mind and senses, the feel of our flesh on one another, the startling clarity of his eyes locked on mine, and the intimate knowledge of the real man who lived behind them. And now, he was gone. How do you fix a mistake that can no longer be undone?

Awhile later, the woman returned. "Here you are, Madame," she said politely when she reentered, disrupting my misery. "It's not fine clothing by any stretch of imagination, but it might do. If needed, I can send someone for a gown."

I stared at the bundle she held. The garments, including a pair of thin satin slippers, were all black.

"Thank you," I said. A tear trailed uncontrollably down my cheek. It moved me that she had known.

She merely nodded then helped me get dressed. The trousers she'd procured were men's, but I didn't care. The tunic, also black, was embroidered and beaded in traditional Moroccan design. Once she settled me into the clothing, she worked a brush through my hair. I fingered the tunic. It was made of silk and sheer material trimmed with black beads on the neck and hem. It hung low on my chest, my bodice peeking out of the top.

"Would you like me to plait your hair?" she asked.

"No," I said absently.

She nodded and helped me to the door.

I stuffed Byron's shirt and the vial of laudanum safely in my satchel. I then pulled out my cap, the lily pin still safely attached, and put it on.

"I need to see Edward."

The woman said nothing but led me down a blue and orange tiled hallway in what turned out to be an ornately decorated villa. Flashes of memory crossed my mind. I remembered dining, sitting on a satin cushion rather than a chair, at a long table heaped with olives, bread, and roasted lamb. I then remembered watching a woman dressed in veils twirl before us, her hips gyrating as she danced, and Edward calling for me to dance with her. I slapped the floodgate on my memories closed. I didn't want to see more.

"Here you are," she said, opening the door to a bedchamber. She stood outside, her eyes glued to her feet. I eyed her curiously then entered the bedchamber which was decorated in the same Moroccan style as my own. Edward was still asleep. He lay naked, face down, between two beautiful, and also naked, women with poker-straight black hair. No one stirred when I entered.

"Edward," I called, standing beside his bed.

He didn't move.

"Edward?" I said again. He groaned but did not answer. Carefully, I leaned over one of the sleeping girls and kissed him lightly on the cheek. "Thank you," I whispered.

"Lily?" he moaned but did not stir.

I looked out Edward's window. The airship towers were not so far away. I could make out a dozen or more ships anchored on the platforms. It was time to go. I left the room quietly and rejoined the woman who waited in the hall. I nodded to her.

"Very well, Madame," she said then led me silently back through the villa.

We passed an open interior garden. A peacock called, its feathers fanning in alarm as we walked by. Again, disconnected memories fluttered through my mind. I remembered sitting in the open space smoking opium and staring at the stars overhead. I also remembered a large fire burning in the center of the garden. Edward's cheeks had glowed red as he'd tossed Byron's journals into the flames.

"Here you are," the woman said at last, pushing open a door to the courtyard outside. There I found a rider dressed in a dark blue djellaba waiting on a black Barbary horse. "You will be taken to the airship towers," she said.

The rider, whose face was shadowed by his hood and dark glasses, lent me a hand to help me mount behind him. The woman ensured I had a good grip on my satchel then went back inside, her black robes trailing behind her. Clicking his tongue, the rider spurred his horse down the dusty road away from the villa toward the airship towers.

The towers sat adjacent to the sailing ships docked in the Atlantic. As it turned out, I was in Casablanca. I'd never been there before, and not remembering anything about the time I'd spent there just now, I guess I still had never really been there. The rider left me at the boardwalk. I was overcome by the briny smell of the sea. A strong wind blew. I could taste the salt in the air. Overhead, sea birds called to one another. I pulled on my dark glasses and made my way through the crowd toward the stationmaster's office. I eyed the ships docked overhead. While the airship towers were crowded, I didn't recognize a single craft; the ships overhead were pirate vessels. Their multicolored and patched balloons and glimmering weaponry were telltale. I steeled my nerve.

Though it was still early morning, the loud-mouthed pirates were already arguing, some brawling, on the boardwalk. Perhaps, given how it early it was, they were *still* brawling.

I was walking down the boardwalk, the planks rough under my slipper-bedecked feet, when a gold-toothed pirate with a thick Australian accent called to me: "Hey, pretty! Why the rush? Why not stop for breakfast?" Laughing, he thrust his pelvis at me. His companions howled along with him.

In my youth aboard the *Iphigenia* with Mr. Olea-nder and Mr. Fletcher, such language had been commonplace. I simply ignored the men and hurried along to the stationmaster's office. The bell over the door jangled sharply when I entered. Within, I found a boozy looking man with stringy silver hair, his two front teeth missing, in no better condition than myself.

"Aye, now, here is a beautiful lady," he slurred. "What do you need, sweetheart?"

"A charter."

"Oh, a woman of adventure? Where you headed?"

I frowned. It paid to be less than specific. "North."

He laughed. "Ah yes, north! Marvelous country. Well, I think Sionnaigh is due in tonight. He tends to travel north."

It was my turn to laugh.

"No? Pleasure cruiser headed to London by way of Madrid, if you fancy."

I frowned.

"Well," he said, thinking it over, "there is one other ship anchored. Lady pilot. The *Orpheus*. She might take you north."

"Fine."

"Decisive girl," he said with a laugh. "All right, beauty. Let's head up." Moving slowly, he grabbed a cane leaning against his desk then led me outside.

We rode the lift up, the metal gears cranking loudly. The stationmaster chatted nosily.

"So what is a pretty lady like you doing traveling all alone? Where you headed up north? Family problems? You look familiar, have we met before? Don't talk much, eh sweetheart?" He rattled on and on, asking me far more questions than I wanted to answer. I ignored his questions, responding only with a look.

"All right, all right," he said, finally giving up. When we reached the top, he pushed open the gate to the platform. The strong wind coming off the Atlantic made the airships wag in the breeze. Crews of mercenary men in their ballooning trousers and wide brimmed hats lounged about their airships. I kept my head low. The stationmaster led me past the larger airships to a small, ornately carved airship whose balloon boasted a harp: the *Orpheus*.

"Hermia?" the stationmaster called.

"What now?" I heard a woman reply, her thick Irish accent filled with annoyance.

"I have a customer."

"Is that right?" A woman with startlingly white hair appeared from inside the Captain's quarters. She looked me over from top to bottom as she wiped the grease from her hands with an old rag. "You alone, love?" she asked me.

"Yes."

She nodded. "That will do," she said dismissively to the stationmaster.

He grunted in assent then slowly headed back down the platform.

"Where can I take you?" she asked me. She stood with her hands on her hips. Overhead, her elderly balloonman watched the exchange. He smiled a wide, toothy grin. His goggles made his eyes seem three times their size, and his white hair stuck out so straight on the sides that it looked like he had wings.

"Edinburgh."

"Oh, well, that's quite a haul," she said. She was bargaining, but I wasn't in the mood. I looked into my satchel, fished my fingers around the coins in my pouch, and offered her half the amount there. It was twice the going rate. She eyed me over, her green eyes assessing, then nodded. "Got a name?" she asked.

Penelope Temenos. Lily Fletcher. Lily Stargazer. Beatrice Colonna. Lily . . . Penelope . . . Byron. Lost. Broken. "Lara."

"Come aboard," she said with a soft smile. "We'll anchors aweigh as soon as the galley is settled."

I boarded the ship and headed to the prow. I settled in the nook behind the bowsprit. Taking out the laudanum, I rolled the small vial back and forth across my palm. It glimmered in the sunlight. I wanted to throw it overboard. I really wanted to. I tried to think about my life. I tried to think about the upcoming qualifying. I knew I needed to be at my best, but at that moment, I didn't care. When I thought about the race, I felt . . . nothing. I took a drop of the laudanum, knowing I was failing, falling. And for the first time in what felt like days, I tried to think about Sal. When I did, I felt . . . well, I was afraid of what I felt.

CHAPTER 15

THE SMALL SHIP LIFTED OFF lazily. I curled up against the rail and watched the bowsprit push through the clouds. The wind felt cool against my cheeks. I felt lost, like my soul had been unmoored from its reason. I was so hollow. When the tears rolled down my face, I didn't really feel sad. I had passed beyond the pale into emptiness. I took out Byron's bottle of cologne and breathed in deeply. It was like I was conjuring up his ghost. My mind was tormented.

Hermia did not try to make conversation. Her quick eyes seem to take in everything. Once she'd got her ship on course, she mucked around in her Captain's quarters, appearing again with a tray in her hands.

"I assumed you drink it with sugar," she said, setting the tray down on the deck beside me. On it was a cup of tea and a plate of biscuits.

Surprised, I looked up at her. I wiped the tears from my cheeks. I didn't know what to say.

She smiled kindly, her green eyes crinkling at the corners. She sat beside me and took my hand. "There now, love," she said, patting my hand. "There now. Keep him locked in your memory. Let him live alongside you." She pulled me into an embrace.

I wept on the woman's shoulder. She was warm and soft. She smelled of lilacs, gear grease, and the wind. My grief terrified me. I wept until I couldn't catch my breath then pulled back, trying to breathe in the wind. I felt like I needed to put the sky back inside my heart. My head ached.

"Drink," she said. She picked up the teacup and handed it to me.

I nodded dutifully then sipped the tea. I smiled as best I could at her. I was so grateful for her sympathy. Satisfied, Hermia nodded then headed back to the wheelstand. The tea went down easy. When I had finished the cup, I looked within. On the bottom, the leaves had again fallen into the shape of the triskelion. I set the cup down, took another drop of laudanum, then rested my head against the rail. I closed my eyes and let the wind wrap around me.

WE ARRIVED IN EDINBURGH ALMOST two days later. When Hermia lowered the *Orpheus* into the docking bay, I could feel my real life insisting itself upon me. I wasn't ready. This was my flight circuit, and everyone on the tower knew me. Word would spread that I'd returned—but not to London.

Hermia and I stood on the platform outside the *Orpheus.* "My thanks," I told her, "for your many kindnesses."

"Mornin', Lily," Morris, one of the tower guards, said as he passed by. "*Stargazer* in port?"

"No. Just passing through."

Hermia smiled knowingly then pulled me into an embrace. "Always liked his poetry. Shame. Good luck to you, love," she said then boarded her ship.

I took a deep breath, holding back the tears that threatened, then took the lift down to the city. Edinburgh towers sat at the lower end of the Royal Mile near Holyrood Palace. I began my trek to the bank. Flagging down a wagon, I hopped in the back. I settled in on the straw, crates full of glass bottles rattling behind me, as the cart clattered down the city street. I kept my glasses on and my head low. It was market day in Edinburgh, and the streets were flooded with people. I stared at the usually interesting scene with almost vacant eyes. The mood on the Mile was somber. A tinker had modified a piper's bagpipe to amplify sound from a very large copper speaker. The piper, aided by a big-voiced lass, had the entire Royal Mile awash with melancholy ballad of *Bonny Portmore*. Nearly everyone had frozen still. I imagined they were all in grief with me. I pulled my legs up and put my head on my knees, rocking with the carriage. I tried to shut down my mind to everything and anything.

As we neared the Bank of Scotland, I hopped off the cart. The bank, a massive building that rivaled Edinburgh Castle in its magnitude, towered over me. Its thick walls, arched windows, and the domed pinnacle on its roof made it look like a fortress. I took a deep breath then entered.

"Madame," the doorman said kindly. He eyed my clothing. Still dressed in my odd, ill-fitting, half-Moroccan outfit, I was quite the sight.

I wandered into the massive open foyer where clerks waited on bank patrons. Since I was still wearing the silk slippers, my feet took chill from the marble floor. Suddenly feeling a bit faint, I swooned. A number of properly dressed ladies looked me over and frowned disdainfully.

"Can I assist you, Madame?" a young clerk dressed in a dark suit asked.

"Yes. I'm here to see the bank president."

He looked at me like I might be crazy. Maybe I was, but not the way he thought. "That requires a matter of serious consequence. Perhaps I can guide you otherwise? Do you need alms? We can certainly-"

"No, you idiot. I need to see the bank president. Tell him Lily Stargazer wants to see him regarding a matter of immediate importance."

"Lily St-" The man looked at me like he was about to laugh in my face, then he peered more closely at me. "Bloody hell, you *are* Lily Stargazer. My apologies, I didn't recognize you dressed . . . like that. Please come with me," he said then led me toward the back. We wove through the narrow, wood-paneled hallway into the interior of the building. Somewhere in that maze, he took me to a small waiting room.

"Again, my apologies. Please wait here. I'll let President Spencer know you are here and will see if he can meet you today."

"Please tell him it's important."

"Yes, Madame."

I flopped onto a red velvet settee and closed my eyes. The bank was deadly silent. It was like the money itself insulated the walls from the noise of the city outside. It wasn't very long after that the door opened again, but I must have drifted off because I was startled by the sound. I sat bolt upright.

Standing in the doorframe was a tall, thin man in a black suit. He wore a pearl-white silk ascot and a serious expression. "You are Miss Stargazer?" he asked.

Trying to pull myself together, I stood. "Yes, sir."

"I'm Edmund Spencer, the bank president. I understand you wanted to see me."

"You're sure you are the bank president?" I asked, Byron's warning fresh in my memory.

He smiled patiently at me. "So it says on the plaque on my door."

"Then I'm here regarding Lord Byron's vault."

The man's lips tightened so thin that they almost disappeared. "Do you have the key?"

I dipped my hand into my bodice and pulled out the keys Byron had given me.

He nodded. "I was expecting you. Please come with me."

Expecting me? I said nothing but followed behind him. He led me down a number of hallways to a remote part of the bank. This section of the bank seemed deserted. We entered a small, seemingly unused storage closet. I was about to protest when he slid his hand along the moulding. After a moment, I heard a click from somewhere inside. A wall panel slid open creating a space just large enough for a body to pass.

"Please," he said, motioning for me to enter.

Taking a lamp from a nearby shelf, he followed behind me then slid the wall back in place. I was standing in a very narrow hallway. Mr. Spencer, sliding carefully around me, took the lead.

"This way," he said.

I followed behind him as we wound through what seemed like a labyrinth between the walls of the bank. After a while, we came to a small door. Mr. Spencer pulled a very old key from his pocket, similar in appearance to the key Byron had given me, and unlocked the door. It swung open to reveal a flight of stairs leading downward.

"Watch your step," he said then led me down the stairs.

I could feel the chill of the earth as we went underground. A loamy smelled filled the air. We were below the bank, under the city. When we reached the bottom of the stairs we again came to a locked door. Mr. Spencer pulled out yet another key. As I waited, I noticed that overhead there was a keystone carved with the initials R.M. encapsulated in a circle. "R.M.? What's that?" I asked.

Mr. Spencer turned, smiled at me, then shrugged as if to suggest he couldn't say more. I shook my head. I was already deeper in intrigue than I usually tolerated. What had Byron left that needed such strange and secret keeping? The old door unlocked with a clank. Mr. Spencer pushed it back on its rusty hinges.

"One moment," he said then went ahead of me to light the lanterns. Inside was a small room. As the lamps filled the space with orange light, I saw there were seven locked doors set off from the room. The space felt like a cave. The walls were made of stone.

The floor was earthen. The ceiling was very low. The place felt very old.

"Your key, Miss Stargazer?" he asked. I pulled the larger, older looking key out and tried to hand it to him. He simply looked it over, not touching it, then nodded to me. He motioned to one of the doors. "Please. Go ahead."

I stuck the key in the lock and turned it. The lock clicked. When I let go of the key, the door opened with a yawn. A musty scent wafted from the room. Mr. Spencer picked up the lamp and led me inside. He motioned for me to remove the key. I took it out and stuffed it back into my bodice.

The vault was nothing like I'd envisioned. For some reason, I'd imagined some massive stone vault with barred windows and stacks of chests. I had missed the mark entirely. Instead, the room was small, dark, and earthen. Inside was a small table with two chairs. On the table sat a quill and ink and three, small, wooden boxes.

"Please have a seat," Mr. Spencer told me.

I sat and looked around the unadorned room. Mr. Spencer set down the lamp and gently pushed aside two of the boxes. The third box he opened. From within, he pulled out a scroll.

"Madame, there are some formalities I must follow if your patience can abide. First, your name."

"Lily Stargazer."

The man looked up at me, his eyes fixed firmly on my face. "Your name," he repeated.

A tremor raced through my body. "Penelope Temenos."

He nodded. "Sign here," he said, gently setting the very old parchment down in front of me. He lifted the ink pot, swirled it gently, then pushed it toward me. He pointed to the scroll.

I leaned over the parchment and looked. There were about a dozen signatures on the sheet. Mr. Spencer was pointing to a space just below where Byron had signed his name. What captured my attention, however, were the names on the list above Byron's. Many of the names were unreadable, but some I was able to make out: an unreadable name with the title of Earl of Huntington, Geoffrey Chaucer, Sir Thomas More, William Shakespeare, Archibald Boatswain—the master tinker who'd designed the first airship and Queen Anne's Tinker Tower—and Byron. "But Mr. Spencer . . ." I said.

"You are the next designee for the list, Miss Temenos."

"What does signing this list mean?"

"It means you will become Lady . . . Warden of a vast estate held in protectorate."

"What estate?"

"You will become the Warden of Arcadia, as Lord Byron was before you."

Arcadia? The memory of my hallucination of Byron's spirit flashed through my mind. "But . . . I don't understand."

"When I met with Lord Byron last summer, he indicated that you were his selection for inheritance of the title after him. Given that your key opened the vault, it seems that the . . . realm . . . agrees with his selection. As you can see from the names of the other Wardens on the list, this is no ordinary estate. When you travel to Arcadia, your duties will be explained to you. This is not an inheritance of blood. This is an inheritance of duty. Lord Byron selected you as his successor. The realm has accepted you as his replacement."

I stared at the list and after a moment, signed my name, Penelope Temenos, below Bryon's. Whatever it was George wanted me to do, I would not let him down.

"We will request a name from you, a designator successor, at some point in the future. The correspondence will come directly from the bank president, no other." Mr. Spencer picked up the scroll, blew on the ink until it was dry, then put it back in the box. "I will arrange for a transport to take you from the bank directly to Arcadia so you may settle matters there—as has always been the custom. Lord Byron did leave two other items for you in particular," he said, motioning to the other boxes. "Miss Temenos, please be aware that in addition to the very large account this bank holds for Arcadia, Lord Byron also arranged an account—an inheritance—for you."

"What do you mean?"

"Lord Byron left you a small fortune. We will keep the account discreet. I understand that Lady Byron and others are . . . negotiating . . . Lord Byron's estate and formal inheritance at the Bank of England in London. There is no need to inform the Byrons or Gordons or anyone else of the existence of these other monies."

"But I thought Byron was broke."

"Well, being the Warden of Arcadia has benefits."

"I see," I said, but I didn't, really. In fact, I had no idea what was going on. I only knew that Byron wanted me to be there.

"I'll wait for you outside," Mr. Spencer said then, leaving me alone in the room with the two boxes Byron had left for me.

Exhausted and overwhelmed, I rubbed my eyes, took a deep breath, then slid the larger box toward me. It was locked. I looked at the lock mechanism and after a moment, I retrieved the odd punched key Byron had given me. I slid it into the lock. After a succession of clicks, the lock mechanism released, and the box lid sprung open.

The box had been separated into two compartments. On one side was a small skeletal figure, arranged and secured by wire. The skeleton was humanoid but no larger than the palm of my hand. I stared at it. The body was fully developed . . . and it had wings. In the other compartment was an equally puzzling item: an intricately tinkered clockwork fairy. After a moment, I closed the lid. On its own, the box locked itself again.

I slumped back in my chair and picked up the other small box. I was afraid to open it. When I did, the contents hit me hard. Inside was a ring. At its center was a large, oval, deep red ruby. The ruby was trimmed by small pearls and yellow tanzanite stones. I knew the ring. I had seen it once before. Byron had purchased it during our brief stay in Malta. By accident, I'd seen him sitting at his desk staring at it. He'd been in the ship's cabin working on his writing, but I'd gotten lonely for him so I'd sneaked inside. Lost in his thoughts, he hadn't heard me enter. I saw the ring but felt like a snoop. I'd left before he knew I was there. He never gave me the ring. He never asked. Only now, I understood why. I took it from the box and closed my eyes. Tears burned. For a moment, I considered putting it on my left hand, but then I remembered what Mary and Tommy had said. I slid it onto the ring finger of my right hand. I gazed at it, overcome with the sense that I'd married a ghost.

CHAPTER 16

MR. SPENCER'S PRIVATE SHIP LIFTED off the roof of the bank and headed south. He passed coordinates to me and the pilot, telling me the estate was located in Nottinghamshire, adjacent to Newstead Abbey. Newstead was one of Byron's great losses. He was just a boy when he inherited the estate from an uncle; the inheritance had lifted him out of poverty and made him a member of the landed gentry, titling him Lord Byron. But as a young man, Byron could not afford the property. It had to be sold, and as such, it became one of many of Byron's missed chances. I stood at the prow of the small airship and realized I was another.

I gazed at the Edinburgh airship towers as we took off. I loved the image of the magnificent airships sitting anchored aloft with grand old Edinburgh Castle in the background. No matter what ship I piloted, I'd always loved flying into Edinburgh. But today, I was running. I would need to face my life soon. People were waiting on me, depending on me. It wasn't right to let them worry. But, I needed time.

The small ship pushed south over thick forests and rolling lowlands. I held onto a tether at the prow and stood in the wind. I tried to take in the smell of the trees and meadow flowers. The perfumed air filled my senses and caressed my body, but nothing could ease the depth of everything we—Byron and I—had just been through.

Despite my miserable state, I arrived at my destination just a few hours later. I found myself hovering above a heavily forested area. The pilot, who'd stayed silent the entire trip, lowered the airship to the tree line and dropped a rope ladder overboard. "Do you need help, Miss Stargazer?" he asked.

I looked over the side of the ship. The airship was floating above a deer path cutting through the woods. I saw nothing but trees. I sniggered. Help? I was being lowered into the green without rhyme or reason, the skeletal remains of a fairy tucked into my bag. Something told me I might need Merlin's help to face what was coming next.

"I'll be fine. Thank you," I said and grabbed the ladder. I climbed down and landed in the mud, my Moroccan satin slippers sinking into the wet earth. "Fantastic," I cursed, pulling my feet out of the soggy ground. The slippers were flooded.

Overhead, the balloon heater fired. The ladder was retracted, and the airship lifted toward the clouds. Moments later, I was entirely alone. It was late afternoon. The sun glimmered down through the canopy, casting slanting rays of light onto the forest floor. Spotting a rock nearby, I leaned against the stone and peeled off the slippers. I took a deep breath and looked around. The small deer path led deeper into the forest. I stood, now barefoot, and thought about what to do. My hands were already shaking, and a sick, empty feeling gripped my stomach. The opium had me. I took some laudanum and looked up at the trees. Overhead, the new leaves shifted in the breeze, and the soft call of birds and buzz of insects filled the air. I looked back at the rock on which I had been sitting. I hadn't noticed before, but carved on the stone was the word "Arcadia." Well, at least I was in the right place. I gazed down the path that led past the stone. Taking a deep breath, I headed into the woods.

The place was utterly still save the soft hums of nature. It was a warm day. The sun was heating the newly awakened earth. The first flowers of spring, lily of the valley, blanketed the forest floor. Their sweet smell effervesced in the late day sun. I headed down the path in hope that I would find . . . something . . . before dark.

The forest grew thicker, the trees very old, as I moved deeper into the woods. The path led me over a stream. I stopped to rinse out the slippers. My bare feet were managing on the earth, but I didn't want to arrive, wherever, shoeless. Fortune, however, was not with me. "Dammit!" I cursed when the slippers slipped from my grasp and floated quickly downstream. Sighing, I climbed up the bank on the other side. My feet were cold, my back was sweating, and I felt like I wanted to throw up. I pulled off my hat, sticking it into my satchel, and pulled my hair into a braid. It felt good to get my hot, thick locks off the back of my neck. Nearby, I heard someone chopping wood.

I dragged myself off the leafy earth, brushing the twigs and leaves from my clothes, and headed forward. The path led into a brushy gap in the mountainside. The chopping sound had abruptly stopped, but as I gazed up at the sky, I saw smoke rising from the other side of the gap. I was feeling annoyed; I was perspiring, feeling sick, feeling lost, and was just . . . miserable. Enough already. I pushed the bushes aside and passed through. On the other side, I found myself standing in the garden of a very old cottage.

The space, almost completely hidden by the hills and trees, sheltered the small house. At the center of the garden, a fire burned under a large kettle. A small barn sat to one side of the little cottage. There were once other small structures in the space, but they were all overrun with vines. The main cabin, with its thatched roof and stone walls, was nearly choked by ivy. The earth was reclaiming the space. Near the fire was a pile of freshly split wood. An axe sat wedged into an unsplit log. I caught the light scent of cherry coming from the cut timber. Surely there was someone nearby.

"Hello?" I called. My voice echoed.

After a moment, the door to the cabin opened. A tall woman with striking red hair appeared. She wore a long green gown that swept to the floor. The hem was discolored from wear. She frowned but beckoned for me to come inside.

"Okay," I mumbled under my breath and went to the cabin door.

The woman stood in the main room of the cottage near the old stone fireplace. She turned and looked at me. "Come in. Your feet must me freezing," she said and motioned with her long hands toward a chair by the fire.

I entered carefully. The cottage was very small and very old. Overhead, clutches of dried herbs hung from the beams. Copper pots and woven baskets hung from pegs on the walls. Such primitive items gave the sense that I had stepped back in time. On the other hand, there was velvet-upholstered furniture in the main sitting room and a fine rug in the center of the space. Beautiful oil paintings lined the walls and new lamps sat on the tables. Such rich adornments seemed out of place in the quaint cottage.

Patting the back of a chair, she again encouraged me to sit. "Don't be nervous," she said. "I'm Ianthe."

"Lily," I replied, and setting my bag down, I took a seat and pushed my feet toward the fire.

Ianthe pulled her chair near mine. "Then it is true," she said, her forehead furrowing as she sat back. The lines did not disappear when her face softened again. She was, perhaps, more than twice my age, maybe the same age as Sal. Upon closer inspection, I noticed that her red hair was liberally littered with white strands. Her pale skin gleamed like marble, making her vibrant blue eyes, the shade of periwinkles, stand out.

"What's true?"

"That Lord Byron has died."

"Yes," I replied carefully, watching her reaction.

She scowled, her eyebrows creasing. "Were you personally acquainted with him?" she asked. The expression on her face and her tone of voice told me she was perplexed.

"Yes."

She thought for a moment, closed her eyes, then chuckled to herself as she shook her head. "And you are the new Warden," she more stated than asked. She rose and went to look out the window. She laughed again; it was a rueful, frustrated sound.

"What is it?" I asked.

She turned and forced a smile. "It's just . . . there has not been a Lady of Arcadia—save myself—for many, many years."

I thought about the list of names on the parchment. While the list had read like a calling card of the most prominent people in British history, not one woman's name had graced that list—that I could read—save mine.

"Lily . . . Lily Stargazer, I presume," she said. "The airship racer."

"Yes," I replied simply. Something told me that it was in my best interest not to say too much.

Ianthe nodded. She smiled nicely at me. "I have seen your airships fly overhead. How graceful they look."

The woman was odd. I imagined Byron there with this creature who both looked and behaved like she'd fallen out of a fairytale. He would have loved it. "Let's get to the point, shall we?" I said. "What does it mean, the Warden of Arcadia? What, exactly, is going on here?"

Ianthe sat again and leaned toward me. "This estate is a very special place. It is essential to the health of the realm that Arcadia remains as she is. That is why the estate is kept in protectorate. The Warden is the public face of this private place. If there are wars to wage for this land, you will wage them. You are responsible to ensure all of the responsibilities of this estate are met. Arcadia has a long history with the Bank of Scotland and its founders. Much of your responsibilities will be handled directly by the bank. But, in the end, the Warden of Arcadia is someone who is selected because their spirit," she said then paused, "their potential talent, speaks to the spirit of this realm. Of course, there is more that can be arranged between the Warden and me. If you . . . desire something . . . I can arrange for that desire to be met . . . for a price."

"Desire something?" The only thing I desired was a strong drink and a transport the hell out of there.

"Surely, when you signed your name to the list, you noted the others who'd come before you. The estate of Arcadia has a long history of coaxing along the talent of its Wardens."

"How?"

"The method is not really the business of the Warden."

"For a price."

The woman smiled at me with almost a sneer. "There is always a price. You knew Lord Byron well?"

I did not like this woman. As she gazed at me, the glow of the orange fire against one side of her face, I found her utterly untrustworthy. Her striking eyes and ethereal frame made her seem gentle and other-worldly. But her words were carefully measured, and the frown on her face told me she was a woman trying to learn the answer to a problem: me being the problem. I did not like her special arrangements or questions, and I did not want to share anything about myself or my relationship with Byron with her. I did not answer her.

Taking my silence as a reply, she continued. "Such beautiful words, no? They will weep in the streets of

London over the death of their poet. He became the icon of the age. His words and reputation will long outlive him."

I eyed the woman closely. The man she talked of, the qualities of the infamous Lord Byron, had nothing to do with the man I loved. I'd never read his poems. I'd loved him for him, not for who everyone else thought he was. But she didn't need to know that. She'd already made up her mind about the kind of woman she thought I was. In her attempts to analyze me, she'd already decided what she thought might tempt me. And she was very far from the truth. The only thing I wanted was beyond anyone's reach. Why had Byron sent me there? Why me?

Just then, the door to the cabin opened. "Ianthe, I found a pair of slippers in the stream," a man's voice called. "Have you seen anyon—"

Ianthe and I both rose.

I turned to find a young man about my age standing in the doorway. He held my lost slippers in the palm of his wide hand. He was tall, blonde, and had green eyes the color of new leaves. He fixed those green eyes on me with such intensity that it took my breath away. And I knew at once . . . from the cut of his chin, the shape of his nose, the red of his lips, and the curl in his hair, that he was Byron's son.

"Robin, this is Lily. She is the new Warden of Arcadia," Ianthe said. Robin froze in the doorway as if he were made of stone. "Lily, this is Robin . . . my son."

With my eyes locked on Robin's, his green gems boring into my very soul, I found that it was now my turn to laugh. George. My love. My passion. Dearest George. What have you done?

CHAPTER 17

"SORRY," ROBIN SAID, DROPPING HIS eyes to my bare feet. "These must be yours then," he added, handing the slippers to me. He did not meet my eyes again.

"Thank you. They slipped away from me."

"I'll go . . . out . . . the wood," he said then turned to go back outside.

"Wait, Robin. It's getting late. Take Lily to the Warden's Manor. Get the lamps lit for her and the fire banked up," Ianthe instructed then turned to me. "We can continue our discussion in the morning. You've had a long voyage. After a night's rest, we can talk again."

I frowned. I really didn't want to talk more, and I really didn't want to stay there, but I sure as hell wasn't ready to go back to London. I grabbed my satchel then followed Robin out of the cabin.

"This way," Robin said, leading me into the woods.

I stopped to slide the still-wet slippers on. My feet were aching. I cursed myself for not thinking to stop in Edinburgh to pick up a pair of boots. I walked silently through the woods behind Robin. He was quiet. He was not rude. Rather, he seemed lost in his thoughts. As I walked, I looked him over. He was tall like Byron, built much the same, save he seemed more athletic. He had the muscles of a woodsman. His skin was not luminescent the way Byron's had been, but was tanned from working outside in the sun. As I walked, I shook my head. I felt like my mind was ripping apart. I couldn't wait to smoke some opium.

Robin led me to what was the most unusual looking building I'd ever seen—if you could call it a building. In reality, the manor was carved out of the craggy side of a mountain. The door had been worked into an opening in the rock. Someone had fashioned stained glass windows to fit the holes in the rocky boulders. The manor looked to be about three stories in height. On the top floor, someone had chiseled space for clear glass doors that looked out over the forest.

At the door, Robin fished a key from his pocket. The key he held was a flat copper piece with punched holes just like the one that had opened the fairy box. Wordlessly, he stuck the key in the lock. With a succession of clicks, the door sprung open.

"Let me light some lamps," Robin said then went inside.

Cool, earthy air effervesced from the place. It was very dark inside, but after a few minutes, cheery, orange light glowed from within. I went inside.

The manor was, in fact, a cave. The space had been widened in some places; small rooms had been carved from the natural pockets of the cave. The floor, walls, and ceilings were stone. The space did not flow like a normal house. Rather, it moved with the natural curve of the hollow hill. Inside the manor, the décor was remarkably modern. Had Byron furnished the space? And there was ample evidence that Archibald Boatswain had once lived there. Clockwork devices of a myriad of functions sat on almost every table. As I passed through what looked like a study at the front of the manor, I was surprised to find a framed, hand drawn picture of the *Stargazer*. In the corner of the drawing was Byron's signature. I reached out and touched the image. I could almost sense his ghost there beside me, grinning madly.

Behind me, Robin cleared his throat. He was also looking at the drawing. "That's your ship."

"The *Stargazer*."

"I saw the engraving of you in the newspaper, when you leapt from the airship. Weren't you afraid?"

"I didn't have time to be afraid."

"You just jumped . . . without thinking it over?"

"Sometimes the right thing to do is obvious."

Robin smiled then. When he did, his cheeks dimpled in a way I had never seen Byron's. "Let me show you around," he said then led me to the back of the manor. "There are large boulders in front of the cave. That's where the door and the windows are. A mason sealed up the spaces between the boulders and the cave inside the hill," he said as he pointed to the lines in the walls and ceiling. "In the very back, there is a door leading deeper into the mountain."

We went to the back of the manor. A flight of stairs carved into the stone led upward. At the foot of the stairs, I saw a round, locked door leading into the cave. It unnerved me. On the second floor were two very large rooms. Both were oval in shape, but someone had worked the floor until it was flat. And both had been transformed into bedrooms.

"This room gets better light," Robin said then, referring to a room on the more northern side of the house. It boasted two stained glass windows that cast a kaleidoscope of color onto the stone floor. Pristine white blankets covered a large bed. "I banked up the fire for you," he added then looked bashfully away.

I smiled at his shyness. "Thank you."

He guided me to a ladder that led to the third floor. "Do you mind?" he asked, motioning to the ladder.

I laughed and shook my head. "I've been barefoot for at least a week and more than three thousand miles. I'm in trouble if a ladder fouls me up now."

He grinned then crawled up. Once he reached the top, he lent me his hand. It was rough and strong. I felt callouses made by hard physical labor.

"Wow," I said when I finally got my footing.

"This is my favorite room too," Robin admitted.

The roof was concave. Roots from a very large tree growing overhead trailed down the wall. Nestled into the roots were small purple flowers. At the front of the room were double glass doors that Robin opened. A warm breeze filtered in. In the center of the room was a large, round, ancient-looking wooden table. It had been intricately carved along the edges. I set my satchel down on the table and stared at its centerpiece, a cylindrical glass and copper case. Within the case was a tall sword mounted upright. The glow of the leaves outside cast a reflection, making the sword glimmer with green light.

"What is this place?" I whispered, turning back to Robin who stood looking outside.

"It is an unusual manor, but all of the Ward-"

"No. What is *this* place?" I said, motioning toward the window. In the distance, little puffs of smoke rose from Ianthe's cabin.

Robin stared out at the forest. "How many times have you flown over this realm? Haven't you ever felt it? The ancient energy? The fey lines flow between the old, sacred spaces. The remnants of our ancient world. Britannia. Here, we are drawn to her breast," he said then looked at me.

Why did I always get tangled up with mystics? I didn't mean to, but I frowned. I tried to wipe the expression from my face, but I was too late. He'd seen.

Robin looked away. "Anyway . . . I'll stop in later to check on you," he said then moved to leave.

"Robin," I called apologetically. I had not meant to hurt him or be dismissive. I wanted him to know that while I understood what he meant, I lived . . . in the real world . . . in the city . . . with the newest steam machines and airships and gaslamps and clockwork devices and lots and lots of people. What he was talking about was something I had felt before. I knew what he meant, but it was not a feeling I knew well or had ever embraced. When I turned toward him, however, I found him standing at the table looking into my bag.

He lifted the fairy box and turned to me. "Where did you get this?" he asked. He'd gone absolutely pale.

"It was . . . given to me."

He set the box down and stuck his hand into my bag again, pulling out my hat. He looked at the lily pin.

"Robin?"

He looked up at me, a strange mix of anguish and anger on his face. Robin then stormed from the room, dropping down the ladder with a jump. A moment later, I heard the front door of the manor slam shut. I looked out the window to see him stalk off into the woods, my hat and pin crushed in his hand.

CHAPTER 18

I PULLED OUT A CHAIR at the massive table. After rooting around in my bag for a few minutes, I found everything I wanted: my opium pipe, a fresh supply of the dried herb, and Byron's cologne. I lit the pipe and went back to the window and sat down. I smoked deeply, my hands shaking, fearing Robin's anger, fearing Byron's reasons, just . . . fearing. I leaned my head back and watched the trees turn to silhouettes against the early evening sky. I couldn't get lost fast enough. I uncorked the cologne and inhaled deeply. My heart longed for what was lost. I smoked again, taking in as much as I could, then waited. It wasn't long before I began to drift. I thought about Ianthe's words and watched the moon move slowly across the sapphire-blue sky. A chill crept into the air. I smoked the pipe, then another, then decided to search the place for alcohol. Surely I could find something to drive the pain away. Surely I could bury it.

I went downstairs and clattered around the small kitchen on the first floor in search of a bottle of anything. I found one old bottle of wine. It would have to do. As I rambled back up the stairs to the tree loft, I paused as I passed the door to the cave. Cool air wafted in from all around the hinges. On the other side, I swore I heard whispering, hissing voices. I pressed my ear against the wooden door. To my shock, the door handle rattled.

Gasping, I moved backward up the steps. When I moved away, the voices receded, and the handle grew still. It was the opium. Surely, it was the opium.

Wine in hand, I went back to the third floor and sat down. I drank from the bottle. It was a beautiful red wine, no doubt some special, sacred, ancient vintage. Mixing the wine with the opium, I was finally starting to feel . . . nothing, which meant I was feeling entirely better. I sat in the window listening to the owls call until I fell into a dizzy oblivion.

The moon was high when I woke again. The room was dark. I was lying on the cold stone floor. The moonlight cast long shadows across the room. To my surprise, the sword at the center of the table still glimmered with green light. It had not been the leaves after all. It was cold. I rose, gently putting Byron's cologne back in the bag, secured my satchel over my shoulder, then staggered to the bedroom on the second floor. The embers had burned low. I grabbed logs beside the fireplace and banked up the fire. I then headed back down the stairs to retrieve more wood. When I reached the bottom of the stairs, I stopped dead in my tracks. The door to the cave was ajar.

"Fuck," I whispered under my breath and as quietly as I could, I started taking steps back up the stairs.

The door began to open very slowly. I backed away in horror. There was no way I could make it to the front door. I was going to have to jump out an upstairs window. A small hand with long black fingernails reached around the edge of the door. From the open cave, I heard hissing whispers. I shuddered then stood frozen.

"Lily?" I heard a voice call. I could have sworn it was Byron.

I didn't dare speak. The hand on the cave door retreated.

"Lily?" the voice called again, and a moment later, Robin rounded the corner, his lamp blazing before him. He took in the scene. With haste, he crossed the room and slammed the door shut, sliding the bolt securely across the lock. He looked at me with an expression of shock and terror on his face.

Trembling, I reached out for him.

He reached out and picked me up, cradling me against his chest. Wordlessly, he carried me outside. Terrified and completely out of my mind, I rested my head against his chest. In the darkness, I saw the dark shapes of the trees overhead. I heard the soft sound of rushing water. A few minutes later, Robin lowered me onto the ground beside a pool. A spring flowed over rocks and tumbled into the small pond. The water reflected the moon overhead turning the pool silver.

"Are you all right? Did they harm you?" Robin asked, peering deeply into my face. He looked frightened. Frantically, he grabbed my arms and looked them over.

"What was that?" I replied aghast, yanking my arms back before he saw the injection marks thereon.

"The little people of the hollow hills."

What the hell? "That was . . . real?"

"They don't usually intrude unless . . . you don't have to go back there," he said then frowned. Robin rose and grabbed some sticks heaped nearby. He started a fire. The air was cold. I shivered in my thin Moroccan garb. After he got the fire going, Robin sat beside me once again.

"You must be cold," he said, urging me to warm my hands by the flames.

I didn't reply but gazed at him. His face was illuminated by the firelight. My boozy head made me feel dizzy. He looked so much like George.

"Lily, I'd come to apologize," he said, and pulling my hat out of his vest, he pushed it toward me. "The pin got damaged. I'm sorry. But I did fix it. After all, I'm the one who made it."

I stared at my hat. The metal pin glimmered in the moonlight. "You?"

"I'm sorry I was so rude. You must understand . . . the former Warden . . . Lord Byron . . . Ianthe thinks me quite naïve, but I know he was my father. When you arrived, it was the first I heard of his death. Then to find you had the pin and the box . . . I didn't know what to think."

"The clockwork fairy? Did you make that as well?"

He nodded. "I only met Byron twice my entire life. When I was a young boy, he'd come to see Ianthe. I don't know if he knew I was his son or not, but I only had to look at him to know he was my father. I wanted to impress him. He stayed a week. I'd been studying Boatswain's designs. I tinkered the fairy and displayed the skeleton as a gift to him . . . a gift for my father. He'd been so pleased. He'd smiled at me . . . it was like standing in the sun. I didn't see him again after that for a very long time. He came once more last summer. I'm twenty years old, but the minute he walked onto this estate, I felt like a child desperate for his attention. He complimented me, actually complimented me, on my tinkered designs. I was honored when he asked me to make something for him: a pin in the shape of a lily. The pin on your hat. My father . . . gave all my gifts to you."

The opium had my head spinning. I felt very angry at Byron. What had he done? Had he known about Robin? Had he bargained him away? But then I considered everything I knew about the man I loved. Mad Jack's lame son . . . what would sixteen year old Byron have given, bargained away to escape his fate? What would that damaged child have traded to change his destiny? I closed my eyes. I felt a tear slide down my cheek. How sad. How terribly sad. I knew then why I was there. I knew then why Byron had left me the box. In my opium haze, I *had* seen Byron's spirit. He told me I would mend his regrets, the first of which sat beside me. Robin Byron. How much he looked like his father.

I took Robin's hand. "I knew your father. I loved him. I love him still. He sent me here, with that box, your gift, as a message to you," I said, realizing the truth as I spoke. "He knew you were his son. He made me Warden here because he trusted me."

Robin looked surprised but thought on my words. Taking a deep breath, he began to weep softly, his hands covering his face. It moved me deeply.

I put my arm around him and pulled him against me, resting my cheek on his head. I held him tight, comforting him, knowing that I might be the only person in the world who would ever console him over the loss of his father. As I pressed my face against him, I caught his deep, earthy scent. He smelled sweet, like the woods: pine and cherry, fallen leaves, loamy earth, spring flowers, and campfire smoke. I pulled back.

"Thank you," he whispered, inhaling with a shuddering breath. He sighed heavily.

I smiled then stuck my hand in my bag. I pulled out my tobacco pipe. I pressed some tobacco within and lit the pipe. I inhaled, my mouth filling with the sweet taste, then pressed the pipe toward Robin.

"I don't think I've ever seen a woman smoke tobacco before," he said then took the pipe from me. He smoked deeply. "Isn't it expensive?"

I shrugged. "When you want something, you'll sacrifice for it."

Robin smoked again then passed the pipe back to me. "Are you sacrificing on your wardrobe these days?" he teased.

I chuckled in spite of myself. "What? This garb is very fashionable . . . in Morocco."

"You were in Morocco?"

"Yes."

"Is that where he . . . died?"

I shook my head then took a drop of laudanum. I offered it to Robin who waved it away. "He died in Greece. He was trying to liberate the Greek people from oppression," I said. I tried to shake the terrible image of Byron convulsing on the bed from my mind. "It was not a good death, but the Greek people count him a hero."

"You were with him?"

"When he passed? Yes."

"Then he must have loved you. I mean, I've heard he had many women."

I smoked again then handed Robin the tobacco. "He did. Things were . . . different . . . between us."

Robin looked curiously at me then nodded. "I'm sorry I got so angry. I didn't understand."

"It's all right. We're even. After all, I think you saved me from being dragged off to the realm of the faerie," I said with a yawn.

Robin turned serious. "You don't know how close to the truth you are."

"Tell me about it in the morning. Right now, the opium has me. And I want to know where you got that skeleton."

"Truly?"

I nodded then lay down on the earth, resting my head on Robin's outstretched knee. "You aren't going to tell me fairies are real, are you?" I asked, looking up at him.

Robin wiped a stray stand of hair from my forehead. "Are you always so . . ." he said, then shook his head at a loss for words.

"So . . . what?" I asked, my eyes drifting shut. Beside me, the fire snapped. The soft sound of the spring lulled me to sleep. My head on his leg, again I caught his woodsy scent. This time I let it in to fill my senses.

"So . . . well . . . at least now I understand what all the fuss was about," I heard him whisper as I drifted off to sleep.

CHAPTER 19

"LILY, WAKE UP," I HEARD Robin whisper as he gently shook my shoulder.

A sharp pain flashed through my skull making me cringe. Dammit. I needed to stop. I needed to stop this. I opened my eyes a crack to see the sun wasn't yet above the horizon. I was still lying on the ground beside the fire. My stomach ached horribly. I hadn't eaten since I was on the *Orpheus*. "The sun isn't even up yet," I told Robin.

"I know. That's why it has to be now. Sit up and drink some tea quickly. We need to go soon if you want to see."

"See what?"

Robin pressed a steaming cup toward me. "Just drink this," he said.

I sat up groggily. I groaned then sipped the tea. The taste was bitter but it washed the even nastier taste out of my mouth. I grimaced.

"Sorry. It's an acquired taste. Take another drink then we can go."

I slugged back the tea, taking deep swallows. The leaves at the bottom had again fallen into the shape of a triskelion. I stood with Robin's help.

"You drank it all?" he asked, taking the cup from me.

"Yeah, why not . . . wait, what was in-"

"You'll be all right. Anyone who can smoke and drink like you do . . . but, anyway, I dried out your slippers," he said, handing them to me. I held Robin's arm to steady myself as I pulled the slippers back on. "Come on," he said then took my hand and led me into the forest. It was still mostly dark, but Robin knew exactly where he was going. He led us deep into the forest. Climbing over thick logs and through beds of ferns, we walked under the limbs of the old oak trees. In the shadowy pre-dawn light, the knotty trunks looked like old, grandfatherly faces.

My head started to feel strange. I had grown used to the sensation of opium. Absinthe was its own monster. But as I walked, I began to feel a strange sensation like my spirit was floating adrift, winging in then out of my body.

"Robin?" I said as I began to feel myself swoon.

"Sorry, Lily. I didn't think you'd drink it all. Just a little sip aids things along. You probably didn't even need it, let alone all of it. We're almost there. Just stay quiet," he whispered.

He led us to a small knoll. Before we reached its top, he whispered: "Crouch down. Stay low." He dropped to the forest floor. I joined him. "Now, put these on," he told me, handing me a pair of goggles.

I was baffled. "Whatever for?"

"You'll need them to help you see. Paired with the potion, they work well. I crafted them using prismatic theory to see the magnetic field created by the realm's energy, but in particular, to hone in on . . . well, just put them on. You'll see."

"Did you say potion?"

He smirked. Again, his cheeks dimpled.

I did as he told me. Once I pulled the goggles on, the forest around me took on a strange incandescent glow. Everything seemed luminescent, glimmering with hues of green and gold. I looked at Robin who was also wearing a pair of the tinkered goggles. All around him was a pulsating glow of vibrant green.

Robin was looking at me. "Orange," he whispered and lifted my hand in front of me. "It suits you."

I looked at my hands. Like Robin, I too glowed, but the color that surrounded me was orange save my chest. When I looked at the area around my heart, it was a swirling mix of dark gray, black, and purple.

Robin reached out and laid his palm on my chest. The green of his aura dispersed the sadness that had settled there. He smiled gently at me, touching my chin. "Now, let's watch," he whispered.

Pushing aside some ferns, we looked at the hilltop. Capping the hill were standing stones. The stones, like so many others dotting our realm, were shaped like an arched doorway: two standing stones crowned by a horizontal stone.

"Watch," Robin whispered. "Watch as the sun rises."

Everything was so blurry. I had a hard time focusing, but I tried to do as he instructed. Sunlight began to shimmer in the distance. The aura around the stones glowed with glimmering gold. When the sun broke over the horizon, its slanting rays shone directly through the stone archway. The sunlight shimmered in a way I had never seen it scatter before. The beams sparkled like they were blown with crystal dust. Then, I saw them. At first, I thought they were butterflies. A dozen or more small, incandescent creatures passed through the light into the archway. They moved so fast, their small wings carrying their tiny bodies. But it was their shape that gave them away. They were tiny and humanoid. They wore colorful gowns; the reds, blues, greens, oranges, and yellows shone with intense richness. They flew around one another playfully. Robin was showing me fairies.

They fluttered about in the glowing light then disappeared through the arch into the unknown.

I looked at Robin. His body was aglow with brilliant green light. He smiled from ear to ear. Looking back, I watched the fairies. The sun traveled higher into the sky. The hilltop flooded with light. The shimmering glow coming from the stone arch faded. The fairies disappeared.

Robin pulled off his goggles and stood. He reached out, helping me up. I stood then took off the goggles. We went to the top of the hill. The place buzzed with energy. The hairs on the back of my neck were standing up straight. Even with the naked eye, I could make out a strange white light glimmering off the stones.

"They are still around us. We just can't see them now. Can you sense them?" he asked me. He was staring into the arched gateway.

I closed my eyes. Around me, I felt . . . something. It felt like someone or something was standing close to me. "I think so." I opened my eyes. There was nothing there. "What happens if you pass through?" I asked, motioning to the stones.

He grinned. "We'll leave that for another day."

"One thing though . . . how did you get the skeleton? I mean, you don't strike me as the kind to cage up something so . . . special."

Robin shrugged. "She came to me. All enchanted things want to be truly loved at least once before they die."

My hands involuntarily leapt toward my mouth. I suppressed a gasp. I gazed at Robin who was staring at the standing stones.

"I guess Ianthe will be looking for you," he said with a sigh then turned to go.

I joined him, walking at his side under the canopy of green, my mother's—now Robin's—words echoing through my mind.

CHAPTER 20

WHEN WE NEARED IANTHE'S COTTAGE, Robin fell silent. His smile faded, his eyes cast toward the ground.

"Robin," I said, taking him gently by the arm. "Thank you for showing me. It was amazing."

He smiled at me, his green eyes searching my face. "No, thank you. Your words, they've brought me so much comfort." He sighed heavily. "Lily, Ianthe will try to . . ." he said then frowned. He shook his head. "Just be true to yourself," he added then went to the cabin door. "Ianthe?" he called with a knock as he pushed the door open.

"Robin! Where is Lily?" she scolded, her voice full of fury.

"I'm here," I said flatly. Robin and I went inside.

"Oh. Very good. I was quite worried. Thank you, Robin. I need to meet Lily alone," she said dismissively, escorting him back outside. The gesture made me angry.

"Ianthe," Robin said, his voice was low, but I could hear that he was annoyed, "it might be wise to go cautiously." He gazed back at me. "The little people of the hollow hills were out last night," he added in a low undertone. He thought I would not hear. Realizing I'd picked up on his words, he stepped outside. Ianthe followed him. I could no longer make out their words, but Robin's tone was firm. Ianthe sounded frustrated.

I plopped down in a chair beside the fire and closed my eyes. My head felt so strange. It was like waves were crashing through my mind. When I opened my eyes, I looked at the chair across from me and saw Byron sitting there. I saw him and saw through him all at once. He smiled at me, lifted one finger to his lips, then arched his eyebrow playfully at me.

"Lily . . . can I get you something? Food? Drink?" Ianthe asked when she rejoined me. I looked up at her, shook my head, then looked back at the chair.

Ianthe sat across from me, displacing Byron's spirit. "When we last spoke, I mentioned that I can be of great personal help to you: your racing career, your personal life, any struggles you are facing. I can help you, in spite of whatever fantasies my son is coming up with," she said with a shake of the head. "My role here is to assist the Warden," Ianthe said nicely. "How can I assist you?"

Having known this conversation was coming, I had considered Ianthe's words since leaving her the night before. "You said that Wardens are chosen because of their quality of spirit. You said they are chosen because their spirit resonates with the realm. Is that right?"

"Yes, that's correct."

"And that is the sole criteria against which the Warden is selected?"

Ianthe nodded. "Naturally, some of these talents must be nurtured. Sometimes the spirit needs to be drawn forth, or maybe the Warden needs something or wants something. That is where I can help."

"But, if I understood rightly, such an agreement is not required. If I followed the chain correctly, the preceding Warden nominates a successor. Mr. Spencer suggested that if the vault opens, the realm is in agreement. The successor signs their name then becomes Warden of Arcadia in protectorate. Protecting the estate is the sole duty of the Warden, correct?"

Ianthe gave me that strange lopsided smile again. "Yes, in bare-bones terms. But your relationship with the realm is more than a responsibility; it is also a gift. It's meant to feed you, to connect you with forces larger than yourself that can help you find what you seek. I'm here to make that happen. Surely, Lily, there is something I can do for you?"

"In exchange for what?"

Ianthe tried to smile. "It doesn't have to be like that."

"Doesn't it? I see what you took from Byron. You robbed him of his own son. You took for yourself without any regard to what it cost George . . . and Robin. Who knows what you have taken from others. I am the Warden of Arcadia, Ianthe, whether you like it or not. But I don't want anything from you."

I rose and went toward the door.

"Come now, Lily. Don't be rash." Ianthe stood abruptly. "I can assure success in your racing career. You could become a legend. Maybe your family life . . . or a secret wish? I can help you."

"Why?" I said, turning to face her. "On what authority? This bargaining is a game of your own invention and has nothing to do with Arcadia. Are you so bored here? I can only imagine what you said to young Byron, an unloved and crippled boy. You filled his head with ideas of fame just to get what you wanted. He was good enough as he was! You could have told him that instead of setting him on fire with a dream that burned him alive from the inside. The heavens forbid anyone actually love that man for who he really was! Shame on you! I don't need you! I love my country and will shelter this place, whatever that means, because that is what the realm asks of me. But I don't need anything from you. I make my own fate," I said then left, slamming the door behind me.

Full of fury, I left the cottage in a huff and set off down the deer path the way I had come. The longer I walked, the angrier I became. I cursed everyone who had ever crossed Byron's path: from his drunk, half-pirate father to his neurotic mother to his vulture cousins to his manipulative, shrewish ex-wife. I cursed them all. When I was done cursing them, I cursed Byron. What kind of man abandons his children in pursuit of pleasure? What kind of man bargains away his only son? And even if he had been manipulated—which surely he had been—when he was old enough to know better, why hadn't he done right by Robin? Furthermore, I knew Annabella was a wretched waste of life, but young Ada was a sweet, smart, beautiful child. Didn't she deserve more from her father? I cursed Ianthe and the games women play when they grow bored. And most of all, I cursed myself because I was drunk again, strung out on opium, and lost in Byron's world, a million miles from Sal, the *Stargazer*, and Jessup and Angus. I wanted to kill myself.

I sat down with my back against a tree and wept. In my fit of rage, I had veered off the deer path. I was totally lost. And in that moment, I just didn't care anymore. I wept and wept until I was totally exhausted, then fell asleep in the middle of the woods, hoping the little people from the hollow hills would come carry me away.

CHAPTER 21

"ANOTHER INCH TO THE LEFT, and you would have fallen asleep in the poison oak," someone said. I opened my eyes to see Robin looking down at me from his astride his horse, an amused expression on his face.

"Do you have to keep rescuing me? It's becoming cliché."

Robin laughed. "It would be more of a rescue if it hadn't taken all morning to find you. Let's go have a drink."

"A drink? Another one of your mandrake teas? I still have a headache."

"Mandrake would've killed you. That was something else. The *Pig and Whistle* is about five miles from here. They've got a nice bitter."

"Now you're talking," I said, but as I looked down at my Moroccan best, I hesitated. For a moment, I remembered that dinner at Katy's house so long ago. At least, maybe now, I was dressed more like my true self: a total mess.

"And what kind of chivalric rescue would it be if I didn't bring the damsel something proper to wear?" Robin said, as if reading my thoughts.

"Seriously?"

He laughed. "I'd actually gone for the dress when you were talking with Ianthe. Imagine my surprise to return to find you'd stormed off. I didn't get much out of Ianthe. She was still too mad to talk." Robin pulled a bundle from his saddle bag. "What did you say to her?" he asked, tossing the cloth bag to me.

From within, I pulled out a violet-colored gown made of soft chemise material. It was not air jockey wear, but it was a fine dress. "Where did you find this?" I asked.

"The fairies sewed it for me. Out of gossamer, of course," he replied teasingly.

"All right," I said, chuckling in spite of myself. "Well, be chivalric a bit longer and turn your horse around so I can get changed."

"Watch out for the poison oak."

"I did get some on my arm. It's burning like hell."

"We can get you some salve."

"After the pint," I said, and I began to shimmy out of the sticky, filthy, black clothes. Moments later, I found myself standing almost entirely naked in the woods. I turned around and looked back toward

Robin. He was dutifully facing away. I slid the gown on.

"After the pint? Now, that is dedication."

"Any chance you found a pair of boots?"

I picked up the slippers. They had ripped down the sides and were totally unwearable. I bundled them up with my old clothes.

"Sorry."

"All right. How is this?" I asked, turning to face him.

Robin turned then smiled. His expression was appreciative. "Beautiful. Now, give me your hand."

I walked, barefoot, across the forest floor to Robin. I stuck my old clothes into his saddle bag, secured my satchel, then put my hand in his. With a heave, he pulled me onto the horse behind him.

I tried to settle in sidesaddle like a lady should, but then, giving up, I pulled the dress up to my thighs. I slid in behind Robin, wrapping my arms around his waist.

He laughed. "Ready?"

I held him tightly. "Sure."

He clicked at his horse, and we headed through the woods. We dodged under the limbs and through the underbrush. A short while later, we came to a cart path. Reining his horse in, we headed off in a trot.

"You never answered me," he said.

"About what?"

"What you said to Ianthe that made her so angry."

"I wouldn't bargain with her."

Robin was quiet for a while then said, "Maybe that's another reason."

"Another reason for what?"

"Well, another reason why Byron chose you."

I thought about his words. If Byron had regretted his decision to bargain away Robin, then it would have been just like him to make a move to stop Ianthe's game, to punish her. And Byron knew me well enough to know I would not trade away anything. "It's possible."

"You've put her in quite a quandary. I have to admit, I kind of enjoy seeing someone get the best of her," Robin said with a chuckle.

"But she is your mother."

"That doesn't mean I agree with her."

I smiled to hear him say so. I pressed my cheek against his back, soaking in the warmth radiating from his skin. For some reason, being so close to Robin made me feel better.

We arrived at the pub shortly thereafter. It was a quaint little woodsmans' tavern in the middle of nowhere. Because I was shoeless, Robin carried me to the door. He set me down once we were inside.

"Robbie!" a table full of rugged looking men shouted, waving him over.

"Not today. I've got company," he called back.

"Hey, look, our Robbie brought a girl!" the barmaid cried, causing many of the patrons to whistle.

"Okay, okay," he said bashfully.

"We can sit with your friends," I offered.

Surprised, he looked at me. "Are you sure?"

I shrugged. "Why not?"

"All right, gents," he said, then led me to a table where five of Robin's friends had gathered. "Try not to be rude," he told them, pulling up chairs for him and me. "This is Lily," he introduced.

One after the other, Robin's friends introduced themselves while Robin talked to the barmaid. A few minutes later, the woman brought over two bitters and ploughmans' lunches for both Robin and me. I had not realized how hungry I was until the platter of bread, cheese, chutney, butter, and thin sliced meats was set before me.

"Thank you," I whispered to Robin.

"Cheers," he replied, tapping his mug to mine, then we both drank. I polished off half of it, wincing at the sharp taste.

"Christ, Robbie, where'd you find such a beautiful girl?" asked the man who'd introduced himself as Jack.

"Maybe she's clockwork," another man, Alfred, suggested.

"If she is, she runs on bitter," an older gentleman sitting beside me, Monk, said as he looked into my mug.

"Tick, tick, tick," I joked as I reached out for my bread.

The men laughed.

Robin grinned. "She's just visiting for a bit."

"Where you from?" Millman, who sat next to Robin, asked.

"I'm Cornish, but I live in London," I replied as I spread butter on the bread. I handed the buttered piece to Robin then exchanged his bread for mine, buttering a piece for myself.

He smiled at me then took a bite.

"Your people are from Cornwall, aren't they, Eddie?" Jack then asked a wiry man sitting near the window.

He nodded. "From Penryn. What about you, Lily?"

"Morvah."

"Morvah? They got more standing stones than people there," Eddie joked.

I smiled. "We had a small farm near the coast, but that was long ago."

"What do you do in London?" Jack asked.

"Try not to get pickpocketed," I replied, polishing off the drink.

They chuckled.

Robin signaled to the barmaid to bring me another. When she arrived, I took the mug from the woman's hands and drank half of it before setting it down. I rarely drank bitter since it usually made me feel melancholy, but I was trying to dull my aching head. And I was already melancholy. By the time I reached the bottom of the second mug, my head felt better.

"Hey Robbie, I don't think I ever saw you with a girl before," Alfred said. "Gents, how much you bet he's in love already?"

They laughed.

"You married, Lily?" Millman asked.

I gazed down at the ring on my right hand. "No."

"Don't get personal," Robin warned then pushed his mug toward me.

"We're not getting personal, we're just getting acquainted," Alfred explained. "You have a man?" he asked.

I picked up the drink. "Does any woman really ever have their man?" I replied with a wink. I took a drink then slid the mug back to Robin.

"Only until the next best looking woman passes by," Monk joked.

They all chuckled.

The tavern door opened.

"Here's Aubrey," Monk said. "Afternoon!" he called.

I looked back to see an older man at the door. He came slowly over to the table then sat down with a sigh. He took off his hat and set it on the table.

"What is it, man?" Millman asked.

Aubrey looked around at those assembled at the table. "Ma'am," he said to me with a nod. "They are in a terrible fit at Newstead today," he said, referring to Byron's old home.

I looked up at Robin. He gazed quickly at me then looked into his mug. I grew still and listened.

"What's the news today?" Jack asked.

"They refused to bury our good Lord in the Poet's Corner in Westminster. He was too wanton. I guess they'll have to bring George Byron back home to Newstead."

"You heard the news, didn't you, Miss?" Jack asked me. "We learned a few days back that Lord Byron has died," Jack explained to me. "Folks around here are partial to him. Newstead Abby was his home. Where was it he died, Rome?" Jack asked Monk.

Monk shook his head. "No, I think it was on some island somewhere."

"I'd bet he died from syphilis," the barmaid called with a laugh.

Some of the others chuckled.

"No, no, he was abroad . . . got wounded in battle. Where was it now?" Aubrey pondered, running his hand across his head.

"Greece," I whispered.

"There, of course a lady would know, Greece," Jack said. "That sounds right."

"Greece," Aubrey confirmed "That's right. It was Greece. Now I remember, 'cause I heard the girls in the kitchen saying they were going to bury him in the Acropolis, but instead they just took out his heart. I guess they're going to keep it in Greece . . . put it in some kind of shrine. Can you imagine? They took out the man's heart."

"Took out his heart?" Jack asked aghast.

"Put it in a jar, just like the old Egyptian Pharaohs," Aubrey said with a sad shake of the head.

Involuntarily, I stood. "They took out his heart?" I stammered.

"That's what they were saying at Newstead," Aubrey replied. "They're going to build him some kind of monument."

I could feel my body tingle as the blood left the tips of my fingers. I reached out for Robin who stood up.

"Just breathe," he whispered, and wrapping his arm around my waist, he led me outside.

I began to see black spots in front of my eyes. "They took out his heart," I croaked.

"I know. Horrible. Just breathe," Robin said. "Tell Moll I'll settle the tab later," he called back to Eddie who stood in the doorway.

"Everything all right?" Eddie asked.

"We'll be okay," Robin replied then came and stood in front of me. "Look into my eyes," he said.

I did as he instructed.

His eyes were wet with tears. "Breathe," he told me. "In and out. Close your eyes. Feel the earth under your feet. Breathe in the forest. In and out," he whispered.

I breathed deeply, but rather than closing my eyes, I kept my gaze locked on him. My stomach quaked. Staring into his striking eyes, I began to feel better. I reached out and wiped away his tears. His face softened.

"Let's go," he whispered. We mounted his horse and rode off. Robin led the horse into the woods and soon we were trotting along a trail in the forest. I did not recognize the place. I clung to Robin. How could they take out his heart, the heart that had loved me? I squeezed my eyes shut. We'd been riding at a steady clip when the clouds overhead darkened. Soon, it was raining. "We're almost there," Robin said as he guided his horse. The blanket of trees overhead protected us to some extent, but in the end, we were both soaking wet.

Robin led his horse into a thick part of the woods. There, in the center of a fern-covered low area, was an earthen burial mound. Such mounds were frequent across the realm. This one was rather large, maybe eight feet at its pinnacle. Moss grew all over it. Robin rode toward it then stopped. He dismounted then helped me down, leaving the horse to roam free. He led me toward the mound.

"In there?" I asked him.

"It's okay. This is where I stay," he said.

Curious, I followed him. He opened a small, handmade wooden door. Bending low, he went inside. I followed behind him.

Moments later, I was standing inside the mound. The walls were fortified with stones. The curved earthen ceiling overhead was reinforced with timbers.

He'd lined the floor with straw. In his main living area, he'd laid animal hides on the floor. Taking my hand, he led me to a bed sitting along the curved wall.

"Cover up," he said, pulling his blanket around me. I was overcome by his earthy smell. All around the room, he had work stations covered with tinkered contraptions. For a moment, I felt like I was in Sal's workshop. But Sal never had bunches of dried rosemary and lavender hanging from the ceiling nor shelves lined with jars of mushrooms. Robin lit his small fireplace. Soon the space grew warm and filled with the scent of wood smoke. The fire made the space glow with a cheerful orange color as the burning wood popped and crackled.

Robin sat beside me. My satchel was at my feet. "Do you mind?" he asked, leaning down.

I shook my head.

He opened the bag and pulled out the fairy box.

I fished the key out of my bodice and handed it to him.

He unlocked the box and took out the clockwork fairy. "Hold out your hand," he whispered then gently set it in my palm. He took a tiny instrument from his vest pocket, turned back to the box, then extracted a small bone from the wing of the skeletal fairy. "Steady," he told me as he leaned toward the clockwork fairy. Carefully, he set the bone inside an almost invisible chamber along the clockwork fairy's spine. The chamber locked with a click. Then, to my amazement, the clockwork fairy's wings fluttered. Moments later, the small, tinkered creature began flitting about. Robin held out his hand. The fairy landed in his palm.

"Remarkable," I whispered.

Very carefully, Robin opened the back of the clockwork fairy once again. He removed the bone. He gently laid the now-still fairy back in the box and took the box to his workbench. He set the bone aside and turned to his cupboards. Digging around for a few moments, he returned with a blue glass jar.

"The salve . . . for the poison oak," he said.

I nodded. I took off his blanket, my dress still wet from the rain. I located the rash on the back of my right arm. "Here," I said, reaching for the salve, but my hands were trembling.

"I can get it," Robin replied. He carefully turned me to the side, brushing my hair away, and applied the salve. "I'm sorry . . . about the pub."

"Me too," I replied. "I didn't mean to embarrass you in front of your friends. It's just," I said, taking a deep breath as I felt his fingers stroke my skin, ". . . his heart," I said in a whisper.

"I understand. It moved me as well," Robin replied, gently holding my arm. The burning rash had already started feeling much better. He set the jar aside, picked up his blanket and tried to draw the water from my hair. "You're all wet," he said in a whisper. He set the blanket down then stroked the back of my neck.

I turned to look at him. His eyes were the color of green glass.

Robin reached out and stroked my cheek. "Lily, you are so . . ." he began, leaning in toward me.

Confused. Lost. My stomach quaked. I looked away. "Robin . . . I have someone back in London," I whispered, my voice trembling.

He sighed heavily, took a deep breath, and leaned back.

I turned again to face him.

He smiled softly at me, pushing a stray strand of hair behind my ear. He then rose and went to his fireplace. Lifting a copper kettle, he poured me a cup of something hot.

"This time . . . the mandrake tea?" I asked.

He shook his head. "No," he said with a kind smile that evoked those dimples once more. "Never. Always know that you can trust me. I would never do anything to harm you. Drink, Lily. It will help calm you. It's been a trying day. Drink, rest, and be at home."

I drank the dark, steaming liquid. I could taste a hint of opium in the concoction. The other herbs were very pungent and soon the whole room started to spin. I watched Robin go sit down at his workbench, his back toward me. After a moment, he slid everything off the bench with a violent force. The fairy box crashed to the ground. The skeleton broke into pieces when it hit the floor. I wanted to call out to him, but at the same moment, I felt my eyes involuntarily closing. The last thing I saw was Robin setting his head in his hands, weeping uncontrollably. I drifted into unconsciousness, lulled to sleep by the sound of his heart-breaking misery.

CHAPTER 22

FROM SOMEWHERE IN THE DISTANCE, I heard the soft
call of a mourning dove; its whoo-whoo-whoo
sounded sorrowfully. The buzz of insects joined the
chorus. The sun was shining. I could smell new grass
and the light scent of flowers. I opened my eyes to find
myself staring up at a bright blue sky. The clouds were
high aloft and very thin. I was lying in a field,
surrounded by hyacinth flowers. Standing nearby was
Mên-an-Tol, a standing stone monument quite like
the one Robin and I had seen that morning when he'd
shown me the fairies. The Mên-an-Tol, however, was
in Cornwall. I had come home.

My satchel sat beside me, a water skin leaning
against it. My black Moroccan clothes had been folded
nicely and placed under my head like a pillow.
Between me and the stones, the grass was trampled

down. I didn't question how I'd come there. I knew. Somehow, I'd come through the stones. It was Robin's doing, but how, I didn't know.

The sky over Cornwall was clear and bright. My head didn't hurt nearly as much as it had. I stood, looked back at the stones, then turned and headed toward the road. There was so much I didn't know, didn't understand, but there was one thing I knew for sure: I knew my way to my childhood home.

Barefoot, I made my way down the road. I was tired. I was, perhaps, more tired than I'd ever been before. I walked, almost instinctually, down the path that would take me back where I had started. As I walked, I inhaled the perfume of nature. This was the smell I had grown up with. Before everything had gone wrong, before my father had disappeared, before my mother had lost herself, before Oleander and Fletcher had plucked me out of the charity school, I'd grown up in these fields. I had made crowns of daisies and carried fists full of buttercups to my mother who had not yet gone mad. I had sneaked to the standing stones to touch and feel their ancient power not knowing what they were or why they were there.

I veered from the road and crossed a field. Climbing up a rise, I looked across the vista to see the small farm house where I'd grown up. Grass had grown tall around it. Part of the roof had caved in. The place was quiet. There were no sheep in the field nor horses grazing nearby. Just a single, lonely, dilapidated house sat alone. In the far distance, I spied the coastline. The dark blue waves off the north coast pitched and rolled.

I sat down in the grass and opened my bag. I wanted my tobacco pipe. Inside my bag I found my hat. I pulled it out and looked at the pin. The once-cherished item had become bittersweet in its double meaning. I pulled the cap on. I found my pipe and tobacco tin. I then spied a wrapped bundle I didn't recognize. Trepidatiously, I pulled it out. I unwrapped the bundle to find a small round of bread. I had to laugh. What did I expect? When I looked back inside my bag, I noticed that Robin had also packed the fairy goggles. I left the goggles lying in my bag with Byron's shirt and cologne, the bottle remaining, miraculously, unshattered. Robin had anticipated the real concern correctly: I was famished.

I ate the bread as I sat looking at the vista in front of me and wondered, not how—since I couldn't quite get my mind around how—but why, Robin had brought me there. Why hadn't he taken me back to London? Sitting under the sun, the wind whipping past me, the answer seemed obvious. Robin had brought me home to heal.

I finished the bread, drinking a slug of water from the skin, then picked up the tobacco pipe. I smoked slowly, thinking about what I needed to do next, and fighting off the urge to take laudanum. I needed to go back. The race, surely, was soon. I had no idea what condition the *Stargazer* was in. I had no idea what had happened in my absence. And I knew they would be worried. Angus had guessed what would happen. For all they knew, I might never come back, or worse. They didn't deserve that, Sal most of all. I played with Byron's ring, turning it around and around, then rose. I pulled on my satchel, slung the water skin over my shoulder, and headed home.

I was getting used to being barefoot. The soft grass crushed underneath my feet. I approached the old stone house carefully. Once I got close, I could see the place had been abandoned. The door was slightly ajar; I pushed it open. It creaked on its rusty hinges. The house was completely empty, true to my memory. They had taken the furniture long ago. It seemed that no one ever bothered with the place after we'd left. Dried leaves were heaped in one corner. The shutters on the windows had broken. They flapped in the breeze. The massive stone fireplace was empty. The mantel was covered in dust. In my memory, I recollected my mother's little vases filled with wildflowers and an old clock that had been the most expensive item in the house. It was the first thing to disappear when the debt collectors started calling.

The roof had collapsed over our old bedrooms and washroom. In the kitchen, the doors on the old pantry wagged open and closed in the breeze. I opened the pantry door. It was empty save one tea cup. I pulled out the cup. It was white with pink roses on its side and had a very large chip near the handle. I remembered the cup very clearly. I had been the one to chip it, banging it against the table. My mother had scolded me severely until my father, always the gentler one, had intervened. I put the cup in my satchel then headed outside to the walled garden.

Nature will always reclaim what is hers. The roses my mother had kept so manicured, the beds of herbs that we'd kept weeded, and the prim apple tree in the corner had all grown wild. The image struck me. Under watchful care of my mother and father, this garden had been beautiful. The apple tree always produced bountiful fruits. Unimpeded by weeds, the herbs had grown thick. The roses had neatly followed the arch of the garden walls. Now, everything ran amuck. It was all still there, and still beautiful, but it had grown unattended. Without someone to love it, to nurture it, the garden had become wild. Just like me, I realized.

As I gazed around the garden, I was struck with a memory. I crossed the garden to the western wall. The rose vines had grown thick. Trying to remember, I guessed at the right spot. I stuck my arm into the thorny vines. They scratched me, but I ignored the pain as my hands and memory worked in tandem. I was right. Pushing the vines aside, I revealed an alcove in the wall. Inside that alcove was a small, white marble statue of the Aphrodite of Knidos. I reached out and touched her. My fingers, pricked by the rose thrones, left a smear of blood on the goddess. Gasping,

I pulled my hand back. It was like I had wounded the Goddess of Love. The roses fell like a curtain over her, hiding her once again. I stuck my fingers in my mouth; I tasted the salty tang of blood.

The image of the bloody goddess made me feel panicked. Had I killed what the Aphrodite had sewn together? I shook my head and fought away the tears. It was time to go. I picked my way back through the house and went outside. Turning east, I headed toward London.

CHAPTER 23

THERE WAS A SMALL MARINA about two miles from my house. You could always find a fishing vessel docked along the pier, and you could occasionally find an airship docked in the small, rickety tower. To my great fortune, there was an airship in port overhead that day. To my misfortune, it was broken down.

"Pardon me?" I called, leaning under the ship. "I was hoping to jump a transport to London. Any chance you'll have her running today?" I asked the pilot under the ship on the repair platform.

"Not unless you can fix this bloody thing yourself," a surly man replied as his tools clanged against the ship's underbelly. Hiking up the skirts of my purple gown, I grabbed a dolly then rolled under the airship next to him.

"What the hell?" the man said, sitting up. He banged his head on a galley rod. It left a massive smear of gear grease across his sweaty forehead.

"I took that as a challenge," I said.

"Look, Miss, you ain't got no place under a ship. Get out of here before you get hurt."

"I'm not much for arguing while lying horizontal, are you?" Despite himself, he laughed out loud.

"Lily Stargazer," I said then stuck out my hand.

"Are you really?"

"Who else would climb under this ship?"

"You've a point there. Iris Stormgood," he replied, shaking my hand.

I took a wrench from his belt and had a look. "Your bolt is stripped. You're not getting any torque," I said. "Looks like you popped a belt because it wasn't turning."

"Stripped? Where?"

I pointed. "Got parts?"

"Yeah . . . in a bin upstairs."

Upstairs? "Well, go get them."

Iris thought for a moment then crawled out from under the ship. I heard him murmuring to himself as items crashed onto the deck of the gondola overhead. While I waited, I looked over the rest of the galley. The ship was a mess. Either this man knew nothing about airships or had bought a piece of junk. I started tightening nuts and mending bits as I waited.

"What's her name?" I called.

"What?"

"Your ship. What's her name?"

"Umm, well . . . *Hero*."

His hesitation spoke volumes. "Find the parts?" I called.

I heard him murmur again. He returned a few minutes later with a wooden crate full of bits. "I thought we might need a few other things," he lied.

"All right," I said with a shake of the head. He wasn't fooling anyone. I looked inside and pulled out the pieces I needed to do the repair. "Here, hold this," I said, handing the belt to him. I pried loose a cog, replaced the stripped bolt, then tightened the replacement. I then took the belt from Iris and threaded it around the gears. "Pull," I said, guiding his hands. With his help, I was able to secure the belt back in place. "Now tighten that nut there," I said, handing him a wrench. "Turn it to the right," I added.

He looked at me, a guilty expression stealing across his face, then did as I said. I rolled deeper under the belly of the ship, replacing a few other broken bits, as I instructed Iris on simple tasks. An hour later, I rolled back out from under the transport. My fine violet-colored gown was covered in gear grease.

"Now you owe me a drink," I told him then jumped onto the deck of the *Hero*.

"All right," he said carefully.

Once on board, I sat on a cargo bin and started wiping grease from my hands. I eyed the man over. He was wearing very expensive looking grey trousers, a green satin waistcoat, a cheap linen shirt, and flat leather shoes with holes in the soles. No gloves. No goggles.

Iris returned with two glasses of gin. He handed one to me.

"To the *Hero*," I said, clicking glasses with him.

"The *Hero*," he nodded affirmatively. We both drank.

The taste of juniper filled my mouth. "So where did you steal her from?" I asked. I looked up at the balloon. The ship looked so dastardly that she must have limped into my remote corner of Cornwall from somewhere not too far away. Apparently Mr. Stormgood had attempted, unsuccessfully, to fly her in by himself.

"I don't know what you-"

"Save it. You've beaten the life out of this poor ship. Where'd you fly in from?"

He hesitated then said, "Ireland."

"Anyone chasing you?"

"I don't know."

"Well, you sure as hell aren't going to get far flying like this. I'll travel with you as far as London, show you how to manage the ship on your own. You can drop me there then head on your way to . . . ?"

"Denmark. Look, I can't stop in London!"

"Well, I guess it's good day then," I said then stood. I polished off the drink, lifted the empty glass in toast, and with a wink, set the glass down and turned to go.

"Wait. Wait. Okay. All right. I guess I could use some help. But you've got to keep it . . . discreet."

"I'm just trying to get back to London, and I really don't want to waste my time riding in a carriage."

"It's a deal then."

"A deal." All I wanted was to get home. I didn't care how.

As Iris packed up the tools, I crawled into the burner basket, adjusted the burner, then climbed back down. I set the ship's coordinates then went to the galley. It was still a mess, but it would get us to London. "Iris," I called. He shimmied into the galley with me. "Here, I want you to mind the galley until I get the ship out of port and on course. I can manage the basket and wheel for a bit. Once we get cruising speed, I'll let you know. Do you know how to manage the galley?"

He nodded then took the galleyman's seat. "You do know how to release the brake mechanism, right?"

"Of course, of course," he said dismissively then eyed over the levers.

"That one," I said, pointing.

"Right."

"When I ring the galley, release the brake and ease on the propeller," I said, pointing to the levers. "You'll need to give it some speed," I said, pointing to the foot controls.

"I got it."

I shook my head. I went back on the deck and pulled up the anchors. I then crawled back into the balloon and opened up the burners. The ship lifted tiredly. Eying the ropes, I saw the tethers had taken some wear. I gave the ship some altitude; once we were at a pretty good height, I set it on a steady burn and crawled back down. I turned the ship and set course. Then I rang the galley. With a grinding lurch, and after several false starts, the propeller finally kicked on.

"Poor baby," I told the ship, patting the wheel.

Soon, we were cruising. I locked the wheel and crawled back into the basket. We left the coast and were heading east. I took out my compass. It looked like the ship's rudder had been damaged. She was pulling starboard. I adjusted the wheel's coordinates again then kept moving back and forth between the basket and the wheel. I left Iris in the galley where he couldn't do much damage for as long as I could. We were about thirty minutes outside of London when he finally crawled out.

The ship was cruising at a nice speed. It was starting to get dark, so I had Iris light all the lanterns on the ship. He hadn't noticed when I'd lit the red lantern on the back of the ship behind the wheelstand. I then took him through a fast, but accurate, tutorial on airships. In case he ever decided to lift someone's ship again, at least he wouldn't rip it apart in the process.

By the time we neared the airship towers in London, it was dark. I had been fighting an opium withdrawal headache for the last hour. My mood was starting to turn sour.

"Head back to the galley and slow the ship. I'll get her lowered onto an end platform."

"I can't believe you're helping me. I mean, you, of all people," he said, shaking his head. "I feel bad about it now."

"Bad about what? Stealing this ship?"

He shook his head. "No. I'm a scoundrel. That's a fact and it is what it is. This is just business. But . . . I'm sorry to tell you . . . it was me who messed with your ship."

"What?"

"The *Stargazer*. That's your ship, right? I got paid, a lot, to come trim out some parts, mess up the gears."

"You?"

He nodded.

"Who paid you?"

"Well . . ."

"Come on, Iris. I've had a pretty bad week. Shed some light."

"They picked me up in Ireland. There was a suit looking for someone to do a dirty job. Odd chap. Real odd. His hands," Iris said, wagging his fingers, "all clockwork. And he was a Frenchman . . . don't see many of them in Ireland. I only caught his last name: Largoët. I wasn't much interested in the job. After all, we're real proud of what you did in Paris. But money talked and a lot of it."

"I don't understand. Has he got someone in the race? Is he backing someone?"

"The hell if I know. He was rich, in a hurry, and looking for someone he could pay to keep his mouth shut. I did the job, and as instructed, dropped the parts into a crate on a ship headed to Brittany. That was that. Who would have thought that fortune would throw you and me together?"

"You don't remember anything else?"

Iris squinted as he thought. "He flew out on an airship. The *Viviane.*"

"Thank you. Thank you for telling me."

Iris nodded then headed below. After a few tries, he finally got the ship slowed. As promised, I guided the *Hero*, hands shaking with rage, into port on the farthest tower. He wouldn't even have to anchor in.

"Set your coordinates. Give her a little lift. You should be able to steer out," I said then grabbed a rope and swung from the *Hero* to the platform.

"Good luck with the race," he called.

I waved and watched as he ineptly lifted the ship out of port. He took on too much altitude and the propeller groaned as he mangled the gears, but soon he was flying east out of London, his red lantern glowing behind him. As I watched him go, I debated.

He didn't have to tell me. He could have kept his mouth shut. If it came out that he was the one who talked, it could cost him. Then again, what if that had been the *Stargazer* limping across the sky? What if he'd burned my ship to the ground instead of just damaging it? What would he do the next time money talked?

As I headed toward the *Stargazer*, I stopped by the guard station. I opened the door and stuck my head inside.

"Edwin?" I called.

He looked up sleepily. "Lily?"

"Stolen ship headed east out of here. Told me he was headed to Denmark. He's got a red lamp burning at the back. He's choking the galley. Probably won't even make it off coast. Can you alert someone?"

"Of course," Edwin said, surprised. "Hey, Lily. Welcome home."

"Thanks." Indeed, what a welcome home.

CHAPTER 24

I TOOK A DEEP BREATH then headed down the platform to the *Stargazer*. Much to my relief, she looked good. I hopped over the rail and headed toward the wheelstand. I hadn't gotten far when I felt the barrel of a pistol press into my spine.

"Don't move," someone said.

I turned around. At first I thought it was Angus, but a moment later, I realized it was, in fact, his brother Duncan. "Go ahead. At least you'll put me out of my misery."

"Lily? Is that you? Thank goodness!" he said then pulled me into a tight hug. "Thank goodness. We've been worried to death about you."

After everything that had happened, I'd nearly forgotten we'd agreed to ask Duncan to guard the *Stargazer*. My worries about the ship, and Grant, and the race had grown so distant. It was like those worries belonged to a different person, a different life.

I sighed heavily and hugged Duncan back. While it felt good to be comforted, it was strange to feel Duncan so close. It had been years since we were together. He was still the same hulking creature he'd been, time in the military having chiseled him into the form of a soldier, and he still smelled like honey. It's odd how a person doesn't forget. He'd let his hair grow long. And as always, he was wearing a kilt.

"Poor lass," he said then. "You're naught but skin and bones. And from the looks of you, there's more laudanum than blood in your veins. Come sit down."

"The ship. How is she? Any more trouble?" I asked, trying to focus on my *real* life.

Duncan shook his head as he took my satchel from my shoulder and set it on the deck. He motioned for me to sit while he went to the locker where we kept our provisions. "It's been quiet. They've been working almost night and day to get things fixed. That tinker of yours is bloody brilliant. Wait until you see what he's done." Duncan sat down on the deck beside me and poured us both a glass of port. He pressed the glass toward me. "Christ, Lily. You're a shamble. They told me you were off the habit."

I shrugged. What could I say?

"Took it hard, I guess," he said then. "I thought since you were with Salvatore, you wouldn't take it so hard. But then, you and Byron were always something else. I'm sorry, Lily. I didn't care for the man, but I'm sorry for you."

"Well, it's over now."

Duncan looked closely at me. "For your sake, I hope so. And for Salvatore's too. I'd hate to see such a good man lose you to a ghost."

Duncan's words struck me hard. I gazed down at the ring Byron had left me. If I wanted to move on, I would have to let Byron go. I would have to make peace with his loss. I closed my eyes.

"Lassie," Duncan said, "you're a mess. Maybe you came back too soon."

"I had to," I said with a heavy sigh. "The race . . . the ship . . . Sal . . . I had to."

"There's time. The ship is coming along. That lady pilot, Mandy, she's been helping. Yeah, Mandy," he said then smiled and nodded to himself.

It was just like Duncan to try to lift my spirits. I couldn't help but chuckle. "Mandy, eh? She's a good girl. Seems you have a type."

"A type?"

"Don't they say that everyone has a type they prefer? Yours must be air jockeys."

Duncan grinned and stroked his beard. "I don't know about that. I mean, after all, I've never met two men more different than Salvatore and Byron."

I nodded as I considered his words.

"Yeah, but Mandy . . ." Duncan said then started to look wistful.

I smiled at him and squeezed his hand. "It would be a good match. I was always sorry for how things ended with us. It was never your fault."

"Sure it was. It was my fault I couldn't see you would never give up Byron. Not for me. Not for anyone. At least not back then. After all, you were two of a kind. All the rest of us . . . me, Phineas, that sailor you used to run around with, even old James, rest his soul, none of us could ever catch you. We all wanted to love you. That was our problem. We didn't understand why you thought you weren't worth loving. But that's why it worked so well for you and Byron. He was just like you."

I looked down into my wine. The dark liquid caught the reflection of the stars overhead. Stargazer. A soft breeze blew up from the Thames, carrying with it the fresh smells of spring mixed with the scent of the city. The ship swayed in the breeze. Duncan's words hurt, but they were truthful.

"I have to admit, I wondered what that Italian had done to make you change your ways. But I can see it. The two of you are well suited to one another."

"Why do you say that?" I asked, because it was a question I had been asking myself since Missolonghi.

"He accepts you for who you are. Angus and Jessup . . . and me, I'll admit . . . have spent all this time worrying you were passed out in an opium den somewhere. Looks like our guess wasn't far off. But Salvatore said you would come back. A man like that knows not to squeeze a wild creature too tightly or it'll run scared. You need a man like that, to gently guide you," Duncan said then laughed. "I wanted to pick you up and rush you to the altar. Salvatore is smart enough to know, and patient enough to wait, for you to see for yourself that it's the right move."

After what had happened with Mr. Fletcher, I had resisted any move to wed me. After all, Mr. Fletcher, my adoptive father, *had* picked me up and rushed me to the altar. With Byron, save that moment in Malta, I'd never even thought about marriage. It was only at the very end, just as we realized we were about to lose one another, did we find the strength to hold on. It was a painful irony. But that didn't make loving Sal a mistake. It wasn't that I'd talked myself into my relationship with him. I'd committed to a real relationship, even if I had faltered. Now everything was a mess. Byron had made me regret. Robin just . . . confused things. But I loved Sal.

"Seriously, I don't think you should let them see you like this. Why not take another day or so and try to sober up a bit. Get some rest. Isn't there somewhere you can go? There must be someone you can stay with. And where the hell are your boots?"

I didn't want to leave London, but I knew Duncan was right. There was somewhere I could go. There was someone who could help me sober up faster. I just hoped he wouldn't take my asking the wrong way.

CHAPTER 25

I CLATTERED LOUDLY WITH THE bumblebee door knocker. It was already after midnight. God knows what state he would be in. Maybe it had been a bad idea to go there after all.

After a few minutes, the door opened. A disheveled Phineas, his auburn-colored hair and clothing a wild mess, but now moustache-free, opened the door. "Lily?"

"My head's an opium mess. Byron is dead. The British qualifying is right around the corner, and I think someone might be out to get me. I have been barefoot for at least a week, and I need a meal, a bath, a bed, and some kind of concoction to put me back to right," I rambled. "Can I come in?"

Phineas grinned. His eyes sparkled in the gaslamp light. "By all means."

Kent, dressed in a robe and wiping sleep from his eyes, appeared in the foyer a moment later.

"Please fix the spare room for Lily and draw her a bath," Phineas told him.

"Shouldn't I send for a maid?"

I shook my head.

"No, no. We'll make do," Phineas answered.

Kent disappeared into a dark hallway. I heard him curse under his breath as something clattered onto the floor.

"I wish you hadn't convinced me to shave off the moustache. I could stand here curling it while looking inquisitively at you."

"How about I just imagine it?"

"That will work. Come with me," he said then led me through the congested space to his study. The room was chock full of books, plants, and dust-covered bookshelves lined with an assortment of scrolls, tomes, and oddities. He led me to a pale-pink satin settee then shoved a pile of books onto the floor to make a space so I could sit down.

"One time you mentioned you had something to shake off the opium faster?" I asked as I sat.

"A by-product, actually. You've been in the morphine?"

"To the bottom of the well."

"Sorry I missed it."

"Don't be. Misery drove it."

"Sorry, Lily. Were you there with him?"

"Yes. It was not a good death."

Phineas poured us both a glass of brandy. "Then one last toast before we set you back to right. To Byron," Phineas said, hoisting his glass, "who is, no doubt, chasing the skirts of angels."

I smirked. "To Byron." I savored the drink, the sweet alcohol burning my tongue, all the while swearing it would be my last.

"Now," Phineas said, setting his glass aside, "let me see." He went to the other side of the room and opened an enormous cupboard. Inside, I saw row after row of small glass vials. Phineas removed a small, sterling silver vial then grabbed one of his personally designed syringes. "I think I'll take a stab myself," he said as he sat down on the settee next to me. "I could clear off a bit too, and I want to make sure I've got the right thing before I set your blood on fire. Christ, Lily. When was the last time you ate something?"

"A bite here and there."

"I'll have Kent cook us some steaks."

For Phineas, day and night were all the same. It was no wonder he never employed butlers for long. Phineas pulled a cord tight around his arm and stuck himself with the syringe. "Burns a bit," he said as he injected himself. He removed the needle and rubbed his arm at the injection point. "Itchy bugger. It's the right one. Now you."

I held out my arm. I was ashamed to see all the injection marks thereon. The bruises left by the crude instruments marred my skin. "Quite the party," Phineas said as he tied the cord around my arm. "What they hell did they stick you with, goose feathers?

"Something like that, and it was a wake. And I woke up in Morocco," I said.

Phineas laughed. "I once woke up in Japan. Can you imagine? It took me almost a month to get home," he said then stuck the needle in my arm. The liquid burned. "Sorry," he said. He pulled the needle out. "It may take a few hours before you feel the passion start to wear off."

I rubbed my arm. My nose started itching.

"Come on," Phin said then. "I've been dying to show you something. Been playing with it for months. Just got it working the way I wanted yesterday."

"What is it?"

"Oh, you'll love this." Phineas led me to the conservatory. Therein, he had at least a dozen little burners all brewing different concoctions. "You'll have to help," he said, then handed me what looked like a lamp shade made of parchment paper. It was open at the bottom, but at the top, there was a very small hole the size of a coin. Phin then pulled out a large, lidded clay pot and set it on the table. When he opened the pot, the whole conservatory immediately stunk like swamp water.

"Nasty," I said.

"The nastier the better," he replied with a wicked little giggle. Using some long tongs, he fished out a piece of what looked like spongy algae. He lay it down on a dry piece of cloth then closed the lid on the pot. I was glad, because I had started to gag.

"Now," he said, tossing the tongs aside and patting dry the algae. "Now you'll see." He set the algae in a copper pan. Stealing some flame from one of the burners, he set the algae on fire. "Hold it like this," he said, encouraging me to extend my arms out. "Okay, now, steady," he said then centered the pot containing the burning algae under the shade.

I looked in the pot. The algae was burning very, very slowly, but I could feel heat rising from the pan. But more than that, a wretched smell effervesced from the pot.

"Hold it one more minute," Phin said as he eyed the shade and the pot. "Okay, Lil. Let go."

"Let go?"

He nodded.

Carefully, I let go of the paper shade. To my surprise, it stayed aloft.

"Oh baby! Oh yes!" he yelled then laughed. We stared as the algae's stinky fumes kept the lamp aloft. "Fairy globes," he said decidedly.

"Fairy globes?"

"Growing up, I was always told the lights bouncing across the bogs were fairy globes. Nonsense. I'm surprised I didn't drown chasing fairies. Gas. Rotted earth. Slime. Algae. Harness it. Draw out its gases. Now we have something we can use, not fairy stories."

All things considered, I chuckled. "Are you telling me my ship can be powered by fairy globes?"

"You could say that."

"Oh, I will," I said with a laugh that Phineas joined.

"Miss Stargazer, your bath is ready," Kent said from the conservatory door. I had to admit, he looked rather bashful about the whole thing. Of course, if he wanted to work for Phineas, he needed to get used to eccentricity.

"Go ahead," Phineas said. "I'll get Kent to work on cooking us some dinner. Besides, you smell odd, like campfire smoke and pine needles. Where, exactly, have you been?"

"Chasing fairy globes," I said, clapping Phin gratefully on the shoulder. I then followed Kent through the house to the guest bedroom.

The room, probably given its lack of use, had mostly escaped Phineas' heaps of eccentric bits. It was tastefully arranged, clean, full of plants, and had a large wicker bird cage full of sleeping finches. Exotic animal hides lay on the floors; the bed boasted a red velvet coverlet and a black bear skin.

"The wash room and water closet are through that door," Kent guided. "Do you know how long you will be staying?"

"Just a day or so."

"Is there anything I can do for you?"

"I need clothes. And boots."

"I might not be the best person to select-"

On the bureau I found paper. I pulled Sal's fountain pen from my satchel and jotted down an address which I handed to Kent. "I have a friend, a dressmaker, Celia. She'll know."

"Yes, Madame."

"For tonight, can you see if Phin has a robe I can use?"

"Of course."

"Thank you."

I went into the wash room and closed the door. Phineas' Hyde Park home had all the modern conveniences, the best of which was sitting before me: the giant tub was filled with hot, soapy water.

I pulled off the dress Robin had given me, removed my sticky old bodice and underwear, and set the key to the vault on a chair nearby. The key to the fairy box had remained in its lock, with Robin. Sighing with relief, I slid into the water. My feet were aching, and the poison oak rash on the back of my arm had started itching again. On top of that, I had a headache from opium withdrawal, my nose was running, and my body hurt—everywhere. I prayed that Phin's injection would save me from the sweating shakes that always came after cutting the habit. They were the worst part.

The soap reeked too heavily of roses. Given how filthy I really was, perhaps the overpowering scent was a good thing. I scrubbed my dirty hair and body. It took some work, but I finally got all the grime off. I closed my eyes. Moments later, I was overcome with sleep. I drifted off into a strange dream.

I was back in Arcadia. Everything was so green. The sunlight was slanting down through the leaves, casting glimmering green and gold light onto the forest floor. I could feel someone holding my hand. I looked up to see Byron standing beside me.

"Are you ready?" he asked.

"Ready for what?"

"For Arcadia."

"I don't like it when you're mischievous," I lied.

"Are you sure about that?" he replied with a wicked grin, but then he softened. He looked down at me with a sincere expression of love in his eyes. "How much I love you," he whispered, kissing me softly. He then whispered in my ear: "It is the last and best thing I can do."

He led me through the forest. After a few minutes, we came to a space amongst the trees where tall oaks grew in a circle. Within that circle was a ring of standing stones. Robin stood in the center. Byron led me to Robin, kissed his son on the cheek, then passed my hand to his child.

Byron looked at me one last time, his clear, beautiful blue eyes roving my face, then turned and walked away from Robin and me. When he passed the outer ring of the trees, he turned and looked back at me—at us. He lifted his hand then faded.

I looked up at Robin who smiled softly at me.

"Mommy?" a small voice called out. I turned to see a little boy with a wide smile, perhaps two or three years of age, rushing from the forest toward me. "Mommy! Daddy!" the boy called. With the carelessness of a child, he slammed his little body into us, hugging us both with his little arms. When the child finally leaned back, he stared into my face. His black hair shimmered almost blue in the sunlight. And his steel gray eyes shone with pure love as he looked up at me.

I awoke with a start. I was still in the tub, but the water had grown cold. My whole body was shaking. I didn't know if it was the withdrawal, the chill of the water, or the child wearing Sal's eyes that had me so upset.

"Lily?" Phineas called from the bedroom.

"Yeah. I'm here."

"I'm going to leave you a robe. Dinner is ready, but the dining room is . . . unusable. Come to the kitchen."

"Okay."

Still shaking, I climbed out of the tub and wrapped a towel around me. I sat in the chair, clutching the vault key, my teeth chattering. Forcing myself to get up, I went into the bedroom where a fire burned brightly. I sat down in front of the flame and tried to get warm. The dream haunted me. After several minutes, the shaking subsided. I got up and went to the bed. There, Phineas had laid out a black silk robe with a stitched dragon design. I pulled it on then went to the mirrored dressing table to look for a comb. The reflection staring back at me was a ghost of the woman who had left London en route to Greece. I had lost my glamour. I combed my hair, pulling it back into a simple braid, then lay my head down on my arms. It was just a dream, I reminded myself. It was just a dream.

I stowed the vault key in my bag then headed down the hallway to the kitchen. The smell of meat and butter wafted through the house. I was grateful. All I wanted was something to eat and a soft bed.

"Sit down, sit down," Phineas called excitedly then dropped into the seat across from me.

Kent, who looked as exhausted as I felt, set plates before Phineas and me. Two massive cuts of beef, sautéed mushrooms, black bread, and berry compote heaped the platter. "Anything else, Sir?"

"No. No. I've got it from here. Head back to bed, man. It's late."

"Actually, it's quite early," Kent replied absently then wandered out of the room. Poor man.

"Eat, Lily. My god, you smell a lot better."

"I feel better too. I got into some poison oak. Do you have anything for that?"

"Sure, sure. Poison oak? Where have you been roving?"

"If I told you, you wouldn't believe me."

"I've been roving a bit myself these past weeks since you left. I can tell you, it does not seem to be

Grant who went after your ship, at least not directly," he said then stuck a hunk of beef into his mouth.

"By dumb luck, I leaned the same. What do you know?" I asked, taking a bite of bread. I hoped my body would tolerate the food.

"First I investigated the burning of the *Ruby*," Phineas said, referring to Mandy's ship, his mouth full of food. "From what I could see of the burn patterns, it was accidental. There was no connection to what happened with your ship," he added, stopping to sip some red wine, then he continued, "after snooping around a bit, I also learned that someone for hire went after the *Stargazer*. I tracked him back to Dublin."

I then told Phineas about Iris and the information the scoundrel had shared with me. It was not like the man was even a bit trustworthy, but I did believe he had worked over the *Stargazer*. The rest, I wasn't sure about.

"Largoët," Phineas repeated. "But you're practically a national hero in France after that stunt with Etienne. Whose team do they back?"

"I don't know."

"Then that is what we need to find out. You need to know if they were after the technology or after you."

I nodded.

Phineas then turned the conversation to his algae distillation and how he might reconfigure the burners on the *Stargazer* to use his heating source: ". . . it seems the noxious gas emitted from the algae . . ." he was explaining when I tried to focus, but I failed. While I was intrigued, at some point I must have fallen asleep because I woke with a start when my fork fell from my hand onto my plate.

"Bloody hell, I've talked you to death," Phineas said with a laugh. "Let me see you to bed." Taking my arm, he led me back through this maze of a house to the guest bedroom. Exhausted, I climbed into the bed. Phin pulled up the covers.

"I don't suppose you want any company?" he asked with a grin.

"Seriously?" I replied, half laughing, my eyes already closing.

"Oh, one other thing," he said. "I found the grave for that woman from Southwark. I can take you, if you like."

I opened my eyes and looked up at the ceiling. After everything that had happened, after the trauma I had just lived through, my mother's death felt so distant. "Sometime . . . later . . . but thank you for looking into it."

"Anything you need, Lily. Get some rest," Phineas said then left, taking the lamp with him.

The room became saturated with an aura of gray as the first light of day glowed just below the horizon. The little finches woke and began to sing softly as I slowly drifted to sleep.

CHAPTER 26

REGRET. BYRON SAID HE WAS awash with regret. His death had taught me that I'd loved him far more than I realized. Not having realized it sooner was my regret. As I thought about regret, I realized two things: it was in my hand to mend some things for Byron and that I didn't want to live as Byron had, with a lifetime full of things unsaid or undone. What would I regret if I died tomorrow?

When I woke, the sun was just beginning to dip below the horizon. Night had come again. Orange light poured through the curtains and shone on the palm plants. Their green leaves shimmered in the light. The image made me think of Robin. I sighed. The soft sound of cello music filled Phin's house. I gazed out the window. The clouds were ablaze with pink and orange. I always loved to fly into a sunset like that. The feeling of the last light of day falling on you was magical. I needed to get back in the air.

On the dresser, someone had left two packages. Forcing myself to get up, I investigated. Therein, I found a change of clothing and, thankfully, a pair of boots. I stared at the garments. It was almost like someone had given myself back to me. I pulled on fresh undergarments and a pair of tan and black striped trousers. I also donned a loose silk blouse and a tan vest with pockets inside and out. I slid on a pair of thick stockings then tried the boots. My feet were still a little swollen, but the boots fit well. From inside my bag, I dug out my cap and tossed it on. I felt entirely more like myself.

I remembered Phineas giving me an injection earlier that day, but I'd felt too exhausted to move. Physically, I still felt terrible, but not as terrible as I usually did when coming off an opium binge. My muscles hurt, my head ached, and I was nauseous, but overall, Phin's injections had worked. I picked up my bag then followed the sound of the cello to Phineas' study where he sat playing.

"Did I wake you?" he asked, stopping when I entered.

"I needed to wake up," I said then sat on the settee. "You're getting good," I told him.

"It relieves tension . . . in a productive way," he said with a laugh then eyed me over. "Now you look like the Lily I know," he added with a smile.

"Thank you. And Kent."

"It looks like I should call for a carriage," he said.

I nodded.

Phineas rose. I could hear him talking to Kent. He then joined me on the settee.

"Thank you," I said, putting his hand in mine. "Thank you for your friendship, for helping me."

Phineas smiled. "Kindred spirits."

"Phin, I have one more favor to ask."

"Of course."

"There is a property in Cornwall . . . I want to know who owns it."

Phineas looked curiously at me.

"That woman in Southwark . . . the man in Portugal. They were my parents . . . my home is in Cornwall."

He nodded solemnly. "I'd guessed but didn't have the heart to ask. Just give me the address, I'll know in a day or two who owns the place."

"And the grave. We'll go. Soon," I said, inhaling deeply.

Phineas picked up my hand and stroked his finger across my knuckles. "I don't know what you lived through, but I know the woman you are now. Maybe you don't need that past, Lily. Maybe it doesn't matter anymore. Maybe you should just let it go."

"Regret," I whispered, "I live in the shadow of others' regrets. I'll put my own ghosts to rest then be done with it."

"Then I will help you, if I can."

"Thank you," I whispered.

He squeezed my hand.

I looked at him, lost for a moment in the kaleidoscope of his hazel eyes, and thought about Duncan's words. Had Phineas loved me as Duncan had? Had he been wounded by that broken part of me than ran scared from him? "Phin, I don't think I ever told you how sorr-"

"No, Lily. Just, no," he said, cutting me off. He wrapped his arm around me, pulling me close. "There is nothing to regret here," he said, but there was an odd tremor in his voice that told me he was not being entirely truthful.

"Miss Stargazer, your carriage is here," Kent called from the door.

"Carriages," I sighed ruefully. "Why don't you fashion a vehicle to run on algae?" I asked as I made my way to the door, stopping at Phin's desk to jot down the address in Cornwall.

"Send your tinker by. He and I can build it together."

With a wave, I made my way out of Phin's odd little house and back onto the streets of London.

CHAPTER 27

Soft light glowed from the windows of the loft above *The Daedalus Company*. I stood on the street and looked up. A lamplighter was whistling as he worked his way down the lane, setting the gaslamps aflame with an orange glow. Overhead, the first stars of the night had begun to twinkle in earnest. A cool breeze blew off the Thames. After all the despair and confusion, I stood there basking in a deep sense of relief.

I quietly unlocked the door of the factory and made my way toward the loft stairs. The machines sat still and ready. The entire factory was tidily arranged. I walked up the steps, noiselessly opening the trapdoor. I did not want to wake Sal if he was already sleeping. I crept into the loft, silently setting down my belongings, then turned.

Sal appeared from behind the bedroom screens. He looked as though he had been weeping. He stared at me as if he was looking at a ghost.

My emotions so raw, I burst into tears.

"Lily?" he whispered. In a heartbeat, he rushed across the room and crushed me into his arms. "Lily," he rasped.

Pressed against him, I could not hold back. I wept bitterly, my whole body shaking. Sadness mixed with relief. Sal was my friend, my lover, and my partner. He was the man I had chosen to be with. Maybe my timing hadn't been right, maybe Byron and I should have been more honest about how we really felt about one another, but the decision to love Sal was not the wrong one. As I felt Sal's arms around me and realized that he too was weeping, all my doubts fled. After Byron, things were a mess. But I still loved Sal, and I knew that would never stop. The magic of Aphrodite had sewn us together, but there was something more: choice. I had chosen to love and to be loved.

Sal picked me up and carried me to our bed. He gently lay me down and wiped the tears from my eyes, kissing me tenderly. He looked tired, like the time that had passed had aged him. I brushed away his tears, smiling gently at him, then kissed him again. My hands were shaking as I was overcome with intense emotion. I pulled Sal onto the bed with me. I felt the desperate need to be close to him. Our hands moved gently, removing one another's clothes, and we fell into an embrace, our warm flesh pressed against one another. How sweet it was to smell him, to feel his warmth and the curve of his body against mine. I felt so loved. We made love gently. I wrapped my fingers in his and kissed his wrists, his neck, and his face. I loved Sal. I truly loved him. After tonight, everything would be different. I would never regret my life with him.

I SAT ON A RUG in front of the fireplace and stared into the flames. Sal joined me, setting a tray in front of us. He poured me a cup of tea, stirring in two lumps of sugar, then handed it to me. I took the cup, then on second thought, set it back on the saucer. I took Sal's hands in mine. He saw the ring on my finger, but he said nothing. I gazed into his gray eyes. The memory of the child in the dream came to mind, but I pushed it away. "Sal, I want to marry you. Not a year from now or even someday. Tomorrow."

He lifted my hands and kissed them. "Then let us be married. Tomorrow."

I stroked his cheek. "But first, there are some things I want to tell you. There are some things I want you to know. I want you to know the truth about everything," I said.

He nodded and looked as if he were bracing himself. It was not what he feared. Not really.

"I was born in Cornwall . . . my name was Penelope Temenos. My father disappeared when I was very young. My mother went mad. She tried to kill me when I was just a girl . . ." I began, then unpacked the whole story. I told Sal about the charity school and what I lived through with Nicolette and Mr. Oleander and Mr. Fletcher. I told him about my chance meeting with Byron that had led to me to owning my ship and being called Stargazer. I shared the missing piece from Knidos, the prophecy that had involved my family line that had prompted me to chase Aphrodite, and of the vision I'd had of Nicolette in the waters near the Aphrodite shrine. And I told Sal how Byron had died so painfully and in regret and how much it had broken me. He listened carefully, not interrupting, simply pouring me cup after cup of tea as he let me exhaust the secrets of my heart. I spoke of the vault and Arcadia and the deal Ianthe had offered and of Robin. But I protected Sal, not sharing with him the grief-driven almost-moment Robin and I had shared. It was, after all, just a fleeting moment. I then told him how I'd awoken in Cornwall and about the trail of my life Phin had been chasing and about Iris. And when I was done, very early in the morning, the man who would be my husband asked me only one question.

"Your future is yours to define. Who is it you want to be?"

I shook my head. All my life, I had lived with a sense of double self. I had come to accept that

Penelope had drowned in the Thames. While Lily had been a name dubbed on an unwanted child, that didn't mean I was an unwanted woman. I would no longer hold back the things that were best for me. I did not want to live with regret. "Lily . . . Colonna."

CHAPTER 28

"You must wait for the bank president. Tell him the message is from Lily Stargazer. Don't give the message to anyone else and don't leave until the message is delivered," I told Henry, Sal's most reliable apprentice, as we stood on the platform outside the *Falstaff*.

"Yes, Miss Stargazer," Henry said, then boarded the *Falstaff* with her other waiting passengers. I waved to Bigsby as his crew pulled up anchors and set off on their morning transport to Edinburgh.

"We are meeting the king this afternoon?" I heard Jessup ask Angus once again. "*This* afternoon?"

"Aye, that's what she said," Angus replied.

"But Lily," Jessup complained. "Look at me and Angus. What the hell are we supposed to wear?"

"That's why she is here," I said, motioning to Helena, one of Sal's seamstresses. She smiled sweetly at Jessup.

When Jessup caught sight of her lovely expression, he blushed and looked down. Helena's pale-colored cheeks burned red as well.

"It's just a suit. Look, we're lucky enough to catch King George at Windsor. And we're even luckier that he agreed to see us at the last minute. Just let Helena get some measurements so she and the girls can get underway as quickly as possible. We already have the bloody suits, we just need them cut to fit your stick figure so you're presentable before his majesty."

"Trim. I'm trim," Jessup corrected.

"Aye, trim as broomstick," Angus said.

"Listen to you. You're getting paunchy."

"That's not paunch, its muscle."

"Gents," I said with a sigh. As usual, they ignored me.

Standing on the other side of *Stargazer*, Sal grinned knowingly at me, shaking his head.

"I don't know how you race like this," Mandy, the captain of the ill-fated *Ruby*, said as she leaned against the rail of the *Stargazer*. The wind rising from the Thames blew her long, red locks all around her. "They've been giving me a headache all week."

"Why do you think I have an opium problem?"

Mandy laughed a thick, hearty laugh, her green eyes crinkling at the corners.

"Thank you for helping while I was gone."

Mandy shrugged. "We gals need to stick together. Besides," she said, turning her back to Angus and Jessup so they could not hear, "once I got a look at Duncan, I couldn't think of anywhere else I wanted to be," she added with a wink.

I chuckled, patted her on the shoulder, then turned my attention back to Jessup and Angus. "Helena will be back with the suits in about an hour. I'll be back by noon to pilot to Windsor. After we have our audience, we're going to meet back at Rose's Hopper."

"Wait, where in the hell are you going now?" Angus asked.

That morning, Angus and Jessup had scolded me for probably twenty minutes straight without taking a breath when I'd arrived at the *Stargazer*. It was only after Sal had insisted they let him show me the new galley modifications that they finally had given up. I'd held back giving them the news until they'd gotten their crabbiness out. Now it was time.

"Sal and I have to go into the city."

"For what?" Angus asked.

"We're getting married."

Angus' wrench clunked loudly on the deck.

Sal laughed.

"Did she say married?" Jessup asked Angus.

"Aye, that's what she said," Angus said then looked at me. After a moment, he crossed the deck and crushed me into his arms. "Aye, Lily. Aye, now. There you go, lass."

Jessup shook Sal's hand.

"It will be a hell of a celebration tonight!" Mandy cheered.

I reached out for Sal. With a smile, he took my hand, and we headed into London where, that day, I would become Lily Colonna.

CHAPTER 29

"Stop fussing," I whispered harshly to Jessup. We were standing on the grassy quadrangle in the upper ward of Windsor Castle. As instructed, we'd flown over the castle and anchored on his majesty's small, private tower in the inner courtyard. King George had agreed to see us but under his terms. He wanted a close-up look of the *Stargazer*.

"But Lil, it's choking the life out of me," Jessup complained as he adjusted his collar for the twentieth time.

"He won't be looking at you anyway," Angus said. "Not with Lily's tits half-heaved out of her dress. How scandalous, Mrs. Colonna," Angus said with a laugh.

"You're going to catch pneumonia like that," Jessup agreed.

"Bloody hell, both of you, stop ogling my chest. Don't you know I'm a married woman!" I joked. "Even if he doesn't hear a word I say, I'm hoping they'll be convincing."

"If I remember correctly, that dress was quite convincing the last time you wore it. All the same, you might fluff them out another inch," Angus joked.

"I don't have another inch, thank you very much," I said then, re-adjusting my gown. After Sal's and my private wedding ceremony, I'd pulled out the dress I'd last worn in New York five years back when Byron and I had attended Katy's party. Thanks to my recent spiral to the bottom of the well, it still fit. I smoothed the red satin once more and tried not to feel nervous. I didn't have Byron's way with words, but I hoped fortune would be on my side. Most of all, I was anxious to be done with it so I could get back to the man I'd wed just hours before.

Sal and I had married at a small chapel near the Hungerford Market. The priest and Sal were friends. The jovial man, who laughed about everything everyone said, was fond of Sal's magnification goggles. With the priest's help, we were able to secure a last minute license for our marriage. By noon, Sal and I were husband and wife. Two hours later, I was on the *Stargazer* en route to Windsor Castle to see the King. It was turning out to be a strange, but magnificent, day.

A footman crossed the green. "He's coming down now," he said, casting a glance backward. "Mind procedure. No one touches his majesty. Never turn your back to him. You do not speak until you are spoken to. And you must address him, at all times, as your majesty. Do you understand?"

Nervously, we all nodded.

"Very well," he said then stood in wait.

King George IV. I had never given him much thought either way until *I'd* come to *his* attention. They said he was proud of us. I hoped so. They also said he was a drinker and an opium eater. With so much in common, surely we would be able to find something to talk about.

He crossed the lawn surrounded by a ring of guards and servants. Rumor had gone around that he'd grown morbidly obese. It was true. His weight burdened him so much that he walked with a cane. His white stockings strained at his girth, and I could hear his shoes squeaking as he crossed the grass. He wore a heavy blue velvet coat with a yellow silk scarf. His hair was thick and white and it overshadowed his swollen looking face.

I dropped into a low curtsey. Angus and Jessup bowed. I could feel my knees shaking.

"My god, what a beauty! You are Lily?" he asked, motioning for me to rise.

I stood. "Yes, Your Majesty."

"And this is your crew?"

"Yes, Your Majesty."

"Angus MacArthur, Your Majesty," Angus said with an odd tremor in his voice.

"Jessup Bittonswaff, Your Majesty."

"Well met, lads," King George said then encouraged them to stand. "Well, Lily, I am anxious to have a look at your ship," he said, heading toward the airship tower. He reeked of alcohol. The footman motioned for us to go forward with the aging monarch. "One of my servants framed the image of your leap in Paris. Clipped it from the newspaper. It's hanging in my study," he said to me. "Quite a noble heart."

"Thank you, Your Majesty," I replied.

"Noble indeed," he added, glancing down at my breasts.

Good lord. We stopped when we reached the bottom of the tower stairs so the King could catch his breath. A servant came forward to offer him a hand. He passed his cane to the young man then shooed him away. With a determination, he slowly climbed the steps. He did not speak again, he was far too winded, until we reached the platform outside the *Stargazer*.

"What is that symbol on your balloon, Lily?" he asked.

"It's a triskelion, Your Majesty," I said. "Do you see how all three legs move forward? Constant motion. The past, present, and future all moving together."

"Always on the run, eh? Well, let's have a look about," he said then headed toward the ship. His fleet of servants moved quickly forward to help him, but he motioned for them to stay back. With a grunt, he crawled aboard the *Stargazer*.

"If you like, this way, Your Majesty," Angus said then, opening the galley and allowing King George to peer below. Angus toured the monarch all around the ship, giving him a look at the basket, prow, and wheelstand. Jessup and I followed attentively behind.

"I never paid any attention to the ship they use to transport me about," he said as he gripped the wheel of the *Stargazer*. "There are schematics in my library of the first ship ever designed by Boatswain. Queen Anne matted them on red velvet. Very pretty. Now, Lily, where does one sit on your ship?"

My cheeks flushed. Jessup pulled a locker toward the center of the ship. From within, he grabbed my blanket and covered the lid.

"Please forgive me, Your Majesty. If we sit on this ship, it's usually on the deck. But please," I said, motioning to the locker.

"Perpetually in motion," he said with a laugh as he sat. "Someone told me you are a drinker."

"I've a few vices, Your Majesty," I said with a grin. I motioned to Angus. Digging into our provisions, Angus returned with a bottle and a clean glass. He poured the king a scotch.

The king motioned for me to sit on the deck. Jessup and Angus, taking their cue, receded quietly into the background. The king took a drink then looked around the *Stargazer.*

"The ship is named after you?"

"Stargazer is a moniker Lord Byron gave me. It was passed on to the ship."

He laughed, shook his head, then drank again. "Now, what is it you want? Money?"

"No, Your Majesty, but I do have two requests if you will hear them."

"Proceed."

"The British Racing League has enacted a heavy toll for teams to enter the qualifying. They've made it almost impossible for commoner teams to compete for placement in the Prix. Companies like Westminster Gas Light are buying the race. The talented pilots who fly over our realm every day, and the brilliant tinkers who design their ships, will soon be excluded as racing becomes a sport controlled by companies."

"Can't these commoners secure sponsorship?"

"Not always. The companies like things done their own way. And as you are no doubt familiar, we commoners are not always inclined to agree. Company sponsorship is changing the flavor of the race. Until now, we were crews competing in a sport we loved. Now it is becoming a competition between the bank accounts of sponsors."

"The East India Company plans to race in the British qualifying next year. They were behind the push for double propulsion," King George told me carefully.

It was a rumor I had not yet heard and an important one. If East India was planning to race, their enormous wealth would secure them the most advanced machine available. Next year, I would be in for a very big challenge. The king had done me a favor by sharing what he knew, and we both knew it.

I nodded appreciatively. "Thank you, Your Majesty. I don't suppose they are in the market for a pilot?" I said sarcastically.

"You don't strike me as the type to bend to a company agenda, Miss Stargazer," he replied with a laugh. "You know, if I remember correctly, Archibald Boatswain was a commoner," the king said thoughtfully as he tapped his ring on the side of his glass. "I'm not fond of this entrance fee matter. I'll have someone look into it."

I was relieved. "My thanks, Your Majesty."

"And your other request?" he asked before finishing off his drink.

"Your Majesty, I'm sure you know Lord Byron was our sponsor. And, perhaps, you heard rumor regarding my personal relationship with him. In truth, George Byron was someone very dear to me. I was quite saddened to know he is not permitted burial in the Poet's Corner in Westminster."

King George smiled at me. "I must admit, Lily, I always rather liked Byron. I did suggest to my ministers that Westminster permit his body. I was told that my interference in the matter was not advisable."

I frowned but nodded. "I understand. My thanks, Your Majesty, for hearing my request."

"Love," he said then stood. "Not one Gordon or Byron has petitioned me on the matter. They just complain bitterly about it in the streets. Wherever Byron is, surely your love makes him prouder than any dusty plaque in Westminster." He then motioned to his attendants that he was ready to go.

I rose, Angus and Jessup falling in behind me, and followed the monarch to the rail of the *Stargazer*.

"Good luck in the qualifying. You have the blessing of this realm! I look forward to seeing what you do in the '24 Prix," he said with a wink then hobbled off the ship.

"Thank you, Your Majesty," I replied.

Behind me, Angus and Jessup bowed.

Without looking back, King George headed back to his castle. We watched him go, all of us taking in the magnitude of what had just happened. When he was gone, they shooed us out of port, which was fine with me. After all, I was a bride. Tonight was my wedding night.

CHAPTER 30

"IF I DIDN'T KNOW BETTER, I'd say this was a penny wedding," Duncan said with a laugh as Angus, Duncan, and I leaned against the bar at Rose's Hopper and watched our friends swinging arm in arm to the fast tunes of the fiddlers. They weaved in and out of the timber columns.

He was right. The reception was raucous. Every London airship crew, most of the tinkers from the Market, Sal's apprentices, and even some friends from Covent Garden had come. Sal and I had hosted our friends for dinner and now most of the tables and chairs had been pushed aside for dancing. Sometimes you don't see how much you are truly loved until the evidence is right under your nose.

"Look at your Italian. I'd swear he's got some Celtic blood in him after all," Duncan said with a smile.

Sal was smiling widely as he danced arm in arm with his young apprentices. He turned and smiled at me.

Angus dropped his arm around me and pulled me close. His dark blue eyes crinkling at the corners, he pinched my cheek. "Well done," he whispered.

I winked at him.

Jessup, who had not yet taken off his suit, joined us at the bar and called for ale. He'd been dancing with Helena most of the night. I'd pretended not to notice, for now. Angus, on the other hand, was not as patient.

"Brother, where do you suppose that Helena is from?" Angus asked Duncan.

Duncan shrugged. "Buxom lass. She looks like a farm girl."

Jessup eyed the two of them over his mug.

"Aye, no doubt Jessup will nose it out. He's been at country matters all night," Angus said with a chuckle.

Jessup spit out his drink.

"You keep dancing like that, you'll run out of energy for it," Angus told Jessup.

"For what?" I asked leadingly.

"Why Lily, for country matters, of course," Angus joked.

We all laughed.

"Enough, enough," Jessup said with a chuckle. "Nice girl, though," he said, arching his eyebrows up and down twice.

We laughed again.

The reel soon ended. Brummie, one of the instrument tinkers from the market, rolled out a wooden case. He unlatched the sides to reveal a glass crystallophone. The long, cylindrical glass began to spin as Brummie's wife pumped a foot pedal. Touching the glass with his fingertips, Brummie coaxed captivating sounds from the instrument. Moments later, he began playing the old Irish melody, *Tabhair dom do Lámh.*

"Speaking of country matters," I said as Mandy, who had shifted into a black and white striped gown, crossed the room toward Duncan. Wordlessly, she held out her hand. Grinning, Duncan went with her.

Moments later, Sal came to me, kissed my hand sweetly, and led me to the dance floor. "How lovely you look, my Lily," he said as he pulled me close to him.

While we were in audience with King George, Sal had made the arrangements at Rose's Hopper and purchased me a simple white gown trimmed with small pearls and embroidered with silver thread. It was an elegant dress. "Fit for a bride," Sal had said simply as he lovingly watched me slide into the garment. He'd pinned a simple white lily in my hair to complete the look. I felt like a bride.

Sal had, months before, crafted us a beautiful set of wedding bands. He had been keeping them aside, waiting for their time to come. On the matching bands, he had engraved two swans holding a single anemone flower between their beaks. When Sal had taken my hand in the church to slide the ring on, I saw him gaze at the ring Byron had left for me. I wanted to take it off, but my heart would not let it go. Byron was gone, but I wanted him to journey with me and share in my joys and my failures. This day, he could share in my joy.

Sal pulled me close, kissing me gently, then we danced to the sweet, echoing music. The song, gentled by the glass, filled the tavern with the subtle, fragile lay. In that moment, I saw only Sal. It seemed like silver light glowed all around him. As I gazed at him, I was taken back to that moment aboard the *Bacchus* when I had truly seen him, heart and soul, for the first time. Through him, I had finally started to see myself.

When the music ended, Sal and I kissed gently. The entire crowd burst into applause. I smiled at Sal then motioned I wanted to sit. Still coming off my binge, I felt exhausted.

"Can I bring you anything?" he asked.

I suppressed at least a hundred different urges. "No, I'm just feeling a bit tired."

Sal nodded, kissed me on the forehead, then went to talk to our guests. A few minutes later, the tavern door opened. Henry entered with Mr. Spencer. Henry led the man to my table. I rose to meet them.

"Congratulations, Mrs. Colonna," Henry said, kissing me on both cheeks.

"Thank you! Go have some fun," I said, patting him on the shoulder. I turned to Mr. Spencer. "Sir, I am so sorry. I had not intended for you to come all the way to London."

"It's all right," Mr. Spencer said as he took off his cap. "I was actually preparing to come to London when your young man called. How delightful that I can celebrate your nuptials. Congratulations!"

"Thank you," I said with a smile then motioned for him to sit. I waved to Regina, one of the barmaids, to bring the man ale.

"We can wait until tomorrow to transact business if you like. I will be in London for two days," he said.

"No. That's all right. The request is a simple one, but one I needed to speak to you about in person."

Regina set the ale in front of Mr. Spencer and a glass of lemonade in front of me. She winked knowingly at me. How many times had they seen me try to sober up? They were getting used to the protocol.

"Then let's be done with it so you can rejoin the merriment!" Mr. Spencer took a small notepad from his pocket.

"The inheritance Lord Byron left for me, the personal monetary inheritance. I want that account divided in half. Please put half of the funds in Ada Byron's name with the stipulation that she does not know about nor receive the inheritance until her marriage or maturity. Not until she is out of Lady Byron's care. After that time, please ensure she is given access to the account."

Mr. Spencer gave me a curious look. "As you wish," he said but added, "but you do realize the money will become part of her husband's estate if she marries, as the law stipulates."

"I suspect Ada will marry well," I said but then paused. "Mr. Spencer, the estate of Arcadia . . . given my marriage . . ."

He shook his head. "Madame, the laws governing the estate in protectorate are set aside from the normal governance of this realm," he said then considered. "Perhaps, as an indispensable part of its governance, one might say."

His words were not lost on me. I nodded. "Regarding the other half of the funds . . . I want the other half of the inheritance held for someone else. His name is . . . Robin Byron."

Mr. Spencer's pen halted, and he looked up from his notes. "Robin Byron?"

I felt my hands shake. I hid them in my lap. "Yes, Sir. Please . . . Robin . . . the account . . . must be kept in discretion."

He nodded. "I understand. Please know that all matters of the Wardens of Arcadia are kept private—those living or those beyond. Is Robin of maturity?"

I nodded.

"How shall we notif-?"

"I'll take care of it," I said. I would see Robin again. Just, not yet.

"If you don't mind me saying, Miss Stargazer. No, it's Colonna now, isn't it? We'll make note of the change. But if you don't mind me saying, Lord Byron would have wanted you to keep something for yourself. Some, even if small, percentage of the account for your own needs? I know firsthand that he was quite . . . concerned for you," he said then gazed down at the ring. I wondered for a moment what George had said to the man. "I believe . . . no, I know . . . Lord Byron wanted you to have something."

In my heart, I knew Byron wanted me to be cared for. But I also knew that providing for his children was the right thing to do. They were, after all, his children. "This is how I want it," I said.

"As you wish, Madame," he replied, taking a few additional notes. He then drank his ale as he watched the revelry in the tavern. He smiled at me. "I think every tinker from Hungerford Market is here."

"You know them?" I asked, surprised.

He nodded. "I also know of your new husband, Mrs. Colonna. Quite a talented man," he said. On his notepad, he wrote the initials R.M. and encapsulated them in a circle. He set it on the table. "Do you remember?" he asked.

I nodded. They were the initials carved above the door in the secret chamber in the bank.

"Someday soon, we'll talk it over," he said then put his hat back on. He picked up his notepad and stuffed it into his pocket. "For now, I must go. I will make the necessary changes to the account. Is there anything else I can do for you, Mrs. Colonna?"

I shook my head. "Thank you for coming so soon."

"Madame, whenever you need us, we will be at your aid," he said then kissed my hand. "You make a lovely bride," he added. "Almost an entirely different person from the woman I met some days back."

I rose and followed Mr. Spencer outside. A driver sat waiting for him on the back of two man velocipede. I eyed the machine. It had been tinkered to work powered dually by a small cylinder compartment and the leg power of the driver. Mr. Spencer slid into a passenger seat. I waved farewell and watched as Mr. Spencer wheeled out of sight.

I stood outside a few moments longer. The sweet sounds of the glass instrument drifted out of the tavern. I looked up at the airship towers, catching a glimpse of the *Stargazer* overhead. The sky beyond had grown cloudy. It looked like it might rain.

I heard the door to the tavern open and shut behind me. Moments later, I felt Sal's arms wrap around my waist.

"Is everything all right?" he asked carefully.

I nodded.

Overhead, the clouds cleared for just a moment to reveal a single shining star on an otherwise black canvas.

"Venus," Sal whispered.

"Venus . . . I always wondered, what did the Aphrodite say to you in Knidos?"

Sal was quiet for a time. He pulled me close. "She said, 'Let go.' At first I did not understand the message. Then, when we met Byron, I believed I was supposed to let you go. I was wrong. I needed to let go of myself to become the man I am now. You, my love, I will never let go again."

I turned to Sal, kissed him, then pressed my cheek against his chest.

"My wife," he whispered.

Overhead, the clouds let loose the lightest of rains. I pulled back. Laughing, I lifted my hands to feel the rain. "Of course," I said.

"It's good luck, my Lily! They say rain makes a bride fertile," he said with a laugh. Scooping me up, he carried me back inside where we were met with cheers from all who loved us.

CHAPTER 31

"*STARGAZER*. MODIFICATIONS APPROVED. PLEASE take your places," the league chairman said as he passed our team. We were waiting on the platform outside the *Stargazer*. Twelve ships were anchored in the western-facing ports of Edinburgh Towers. Four ships, which had been eliminated for running illegal parts, had already been moved.

Down the line, I spotted the *Falstaff*. Bigsby had also modified his ship with the help of the market tinkers. I hoped he would place well. I waved to him. He saluted me with a laugh then settled in at the wheelstand.

"*Comus*. Modifications approved. Please take your places," the league chairman told Grant's team who was anchored in port next to the *Stargazer*.

"Great," Jessup grumbled as we hopped aboard. "I wonder what he's running."

"Don't worry about him. We're going to be fine," I reassured him even though I was curious too. Just because Grant wasn't clearly connected to the sabotage of the *Stargazer*, it didn't mean he wasn't a threat. My instincts told me he knew something about what happened to my ship, despite what Phin didn't find. Also, if he was running with modifications, that meant he was flying faster. Half of winning any race involved knowing the weaknesses of your opponents' ships. I glanced up at the *Comus'* balloon. The image of a gargoyle breathing fire was painted thereon. I'd have to fly like Grant didn't exist. I would just ride the wind.

"Wait, I almost forgot!" I said, digging into my bag. "A gift from Phin," I added, taking out a small jar.

"What is it?" Jessup asked.

I grinned. "Woad."

Angus laughed madly. "Oh aye, now here is something! Let's have it."

I unscrewed the lid and dipped my finger into the blue ointment. I smeared a line across Angus' forehead then down his cheek. Turning to Jessup, I drew three lines down the left side of his face.

"Aye, aye, there we go," Angus said as he did a little jig. "Into the battle and on with the woad!" Angus laughed wildly. He took the jar from my hand. I felt him draw the triskelion on my forehead. "Like a fucking tribe! On Beltane, no less. Tonight we'll rut in the fields and howl at the moon. A pack of fucking woadies!" Angus said then howled at the crew of the *Comus*.

Confused, Grant looked up. When he spotted us, he shook his head.

Jessup and I laughed, but then Angus pulled us all together. We huddled with our heads close to one another. "This one, we race for Byron," he said seriously.

"For Byron," Jessup agreed.

"For Byron," I whispered with a nod.

Jessup climbed into the basket. Angus dropped into the galley and started working the gears. I went to the wheelstand. The league had announced the race map at the meeting that morning. They would have us all over the realm. Setting sail from Edinburgh, we had to pass within a fifty foot distance of the towers on the Isle of Man, fly under a race marker in Cardiff, then make port in London. I set my coordinates for the Isle of Man. I knew the path. We didn't fly there often, but it wasn't a hard flight. I'd have to depend on the *Stargazer's* speed, our own ingenuity, and some luck finding winds. Given the weather conditions, we had a plan. I hoped it would be enough.

The officials had finished checking the ships and getting the teams ready. They extended a walkway from the very center of the tower for the league chairman. He stood at its end holding a megaphone and a small sidearm.

I pulled on my hat then checked the instruments again. The *Stargazer* was ready to fly. I signaled to Jessup.

"Ready," Jessup called down.

"Angus. Chairman on the walkway," I yelled down to the open galley.

"Whoohoo!" Angus screamed. "Like the wind! Like the fucking wind! Ride it, *Stargazer*!"

In the streets of Edinburgh below, cheers and the sound of bagpipes rose up. Their excitement matched my own. My body started shaking, my hands tingling. My heart was beating fast.

"Racers, racers, racers," the Chairman called. "On the count of five."

Below deck Angus yelled excitedly and started knocking his fist on the side of the ship. I started stomping tandem. My heart was racing. Overhead, Jessup got ready. We would need burn and fast. We needed it hot. He watched carefully. It was all on him. The west to east shear would slow us down too much. We needed to get above the clouds.

"5 . . . 4 . . . 3 . . . 2 . . . 1," the Chairman shot off a firework. For a moment, the air shimmered green.

For Byron.

Around us, the ships leapt out of port pushing speed and heading west. Alone, the *Stargazer* leapt out of her dock—upward. The burner roared as the balloon flooded with heat. Like a shot, we gained altitude fast. Grant cast a glance back at us. Shocked, his mouth hung slack. With a laugh, I waved to him.

Below, the crowd screamed, and I heard the cheer for the *Stargazer* carry on the wind. Within moments, Edinburgh towers disappeared. We were above the clouds and the shear.

"Now!" I yelled then rang the galley.

The burner turned low. The propeller kicked hard and within a few turns, we began our move west toward the Isle of Man. On the one hand, we were running blind. There was no other ship flying above the clouds. We had no idea where our competitors were. Below us, they would already be ahead a pace, but that would change quickly. I felt the wind. It was blowing east-west. I watched the swirl of clouds below me. I found a low, flat spot above the clouds. I guided the ship into a channel. When we dropped in, I felt a push from behind. Below, I heard Angus work the levers to get better rotation on the propeller. Sal had reworked the galley to be controlled by levers connected to two sets of gears. The difference in torque per propeller rotation rather than just speed had us really moving. The propeller pushed hard, and soon the *Stargazer* was booking across the sky.

"Yes!" Jessup yelled.

We were running horizontally and running fast. Below deck, Angus was laughing. We were making good time. I checked the instruments and kept an eye out for surprises. This leg would be quick and easy. The sky was a brilliant baby blue. The wind was sweet and crisp. It was not long before we started to near our first marker. As we passed east of Withorn, the clouds cleared. We were about to make our above-water descent toward the towers on the Isle of Man.

"Jessup, what do you see?" I called.

Jessup and I began panning the horizon with our spyglasses.

"Astern! Astern!" Jessup called as he looked behind us.

I looked back. The *Comus* was about two miles behind us. I also spotted Lord D's blue balloon on the *Rose and Thistle*. Was that the *Falstaff* behind them? I couldn't quite see.

Jessup and I both screamed. "Angus, we got it!" I yelled. "Get ready for the tower drop," I called to Jessup.

"On it," Jessup called back.

Angus worked the galley; the propeller eased. I pushed the ship in over the Isle of Man and piloted toward the towers. As we neared the marker, I signaled to Jessup.

"Now," I called.

The balloon deflated quickly as we neared the marker. We dropped fast. When we got close, Jessup increased the burn before we lost too much altitude. We were within distance of the Isle of Man marker. Gathered on the end of the tower, race officials watched us come in. A number of spectators had gathered on the towers. They were cheering wildly.

I guided the ship toward the towers. We had to come in within distance or we'd have to go around and try again. A marshall was holding up a red flag. As I got closer, he lifted up the yellow. Just for fun, I edged the ship very close to the tower. The marshall lifted the green. We'd met our mark. So close, we could see the crowd—and more importantly, they could see us. I waved as we passed by. It never hurt to keep our supporters happy. A marshall shot off a firework to let the other ships know the first racer had passed the marker. Now we just had to fly into Wales without losing our position.

I reset the instruments to hone in on Cardiff. On the straight path to Cardiff were the mountains of Snowdonia. It was just like the league to sneak in such a tricky little problem. We could edge west around the mountains and travel over water or we could edge east, travel over land, then have to fly back west toward Cardiff. Given we had taken the Alps, and given we were just that kind of team, we would fly over the mountains and risk the turbulent conditions.

We sailed from the Isle of Man to the shoreline of Wales. We easily kept our lead. I held the wheel steady and stayed on course as we flew into the Snowdonia region. Despite the turbulent winds, it was a beautiful flight. I kept my hands on the wheel, adjusting the ship as needed, while I took in the view. The rolling mountains were lush with green ground cover. Pristine lakes that reflected the blue sky lay between the mountains. A breeze blew off Llyn Cowlyd, carrying with it the scent of the earth and fresh spring water. All at once, I was overcome with the memory of Robin; the thought of him made me smile.

As the mountain range grew steeper, I signaled for Jessup to get us above the peaks. We were getting bounced around between the mountains.

Grant had veered west away from Snowdonia. As we flew out of the region toward Cardiff, we didn't see anyone. We hoped it was a good sign. Soon, the Welsh city of Cardiff came into view. The race marker in Cardiff was a tricky one. There, the marker required us to fly under a walkway stationed between two towers. As we neared the city, I pulled on my goggles and slid down the magnification lenses to get a better look. I turned the wheel of the *Stargazer* and began to get into position.

"There's Grant, and Bigsby is hot on him! They are coming in just west," Jessup called from above.

"Any sign of Lord D?"

"Nowhere," Jessup called.

"How far out?"

"About three miles."

I guided the *Stargazer* toward the marker on the southern end of the city. The space between the two towers was narrow. On the walkway overhead, I spotted the Marshalls and a number of others. I pulled off my gloves to get a better feel on the wheel.

"Lower, lower, another fifteen percent," I called to Jessup as I tried to align the *Stargazer*. I rang the galley. We needed to reduce speed. The space was too narrow. We needed to go in easy.

"Christ, that's tight," Jessup called.

With room enough for only one ship to pass, anyone racing neck to neck would have to give way for one ship to through. Thankfully, that was not our problem, but I hoped the Falstaff would edge the *Comus* out. Jessup kept his eyes on the tower, both of us feeling the *Stargazer's* speed as we neared the marker. From the feel of the vibration in her timbers, I knew we would slow in time. Just in time.

We were low enough and slow enough as we neared the towers to make the pass. Low and steady, we passed under the walkway between the towers. My fingers were tingling. One mistake and the towers could tumble down. I gazed over the side of the ship. The view gave me vertigo. I tried to shake off the dizziness and concentrate. I'd been getting so dizzy lately, no doubt a side effect of coming off laudanum. I focused, carefully steering the ship through. On the walkway overhead, the crowd cheered. Someone dumped a hamper of lilies onto the deck of the *Stargazer*. The gondola was covered with pink and white flowers. I laughed, smiling from ear to ear, and waved to the crowd. From overhead and below, I heard chanting for the *Stargazer*. A marshall shot off a single firework. We were still in the lead.

Sighing with relief, I set course for London. Now I just needed to fly home. Easy enough. Jessup pulled the ship back into cruising altitude. Feeling the balloon lift, Angus punched the speed. Once again, the *Stargazer* was blasting across the sky.

We flew out of Cardiff, quickly passing over the Bristol Channel, making land once again. We were flying over the countryside south of Bristol when I locked the wheel and went to the prow. I stood watching the trees and grass. Nothing. The west-east current was blowing but not very hard. We were already riding what wind there was. I gazed up at the clouds. They were very, very high and were moving very slowly. Nothing. No wind shears. Just nothing.

"Anything?" Jessup called.

I shook my head. "Not yet."

"What the hell is that?" I heard Jessup say as he looked through his spyglass astern.

I headed to the back of the ship and dropped a magnifying lens. Behind me, I thought I saw the *Comus*, but something was odd. "Are those . . . sails?"

I pulled off my goggles and picked up my spyglass. Behind me, and moving in quickly, was Grant's ship. I couldn't believe what I was seeing. The *Comus* was using sails on both the port and starboard sides of the gondola. As awkward as it looked, the ship was moving fast. The sails were catching the west-east wind current, leveraging it for all it was worth, pushing the ship forward.

"Bloody hell!" I stammered and ran to the galley. I opened the hatch. "Angus, Grant is using some kind of sail! He's gaining on us!"

"Better find a wind! She's doing all she can down here," Angus told me, a worried expression on his face.

I went back to the prow. There was nothing. The wind was in a steady west-east flow. "Nothing! Maybe aloft? Between us and the cloudbank?" I called to Jessup.

"Clouds between are thin and dispersing. Nothing up there," Jessup called back, confirming what I already knew.

"Dammit!" I went back to the wheel and steadied the ship. I scanned the horizon as Grant's ship moved closer to the *Stargazer*. Within minutes, the *Comus* was flying adjacent.

Grant waved as he piloted his ship past. He took a position about half a mile ahead of us and held it.

"I don't believe it! Angus, Grant has us!" Jessup yelled down to the galley.

I went to the prow. I heard the levers in the galley work, and the *Stargazer* picked up her last bit of speed. She narrowed the gap a bit, but I would need some luck to close the gap. I felt like I was watching the Prix slip away from us. I stood and looked at the horizon, trying to think of any geographical features we could ride. There was nothing close by and not much ahead.

Maybe we could get a gust off the Thames as we came into London, but that was a big maybe and surely Grant knew that trick as well as I did.

"You'd better think of something fast," Jessup called down.

I glanced over the starboard side of the ship. In the far distance, I saw Stanton Drew, a massive circle of nearly thirty standing stones with two other rings of stones nearby. As I gazed at the stones, I saw something glimmering in the sky. The small thing struggled to catch pace with the *Stargazer*, but moments later, the clockwork fairy was fluttering in front of me. She motioned again and again to the stones. I scanned for Robin. There was no one, just the stones and the fairy. The clockwork fairy fluttered away, flying back toward the ring. After considering for a moment, I closed my eyes and tried to feel the energy around me. I looked back at the stones and squinted my eyes; when I did so, I could have sworn I saw shimmering light emanating from the ring.

"I know what to do," I whispered. "I know what to do!" I shouted. I ran to my bag, quickly rooting through my belongings.

"Hurry!" Jessup yelled.

From the bottom of my bag, carefully wrapped in Byron's shirt, I pulled out the fairy goggles. I pulled them on and ran to the side of the ship. Three lines of glowing golden light emanated from the stones. One moved north-east toward Arcadia. One moved south-east toward Stonehenge. The third line passed east toward London. The fey lines. The flowing energy of the realm.

"Angus, cruising speed," I called.

"What!" Angus stuck his head out of the galley. "What! And what the fuck are you wearing?"

"I know what to do. Jessup, hold tight. I know what to do," I said then steered the ship toward the fey line.

"Lily?" Jessup called.

"Lily!" Angus echoed.

"What is she doing?" Jessup called to Angus. "Lily, you are taking us off course!"

"Just hold on," I called. "Robin, I hope you're right," I whispered.

When the *Stargazer* settled in above the glow of the fey line, it was like someone tugged the ship by the nose. The *Stargazer* hurled forward with tremendous speed. In the basket above, Jessup pitched sideways, losing his footing.

"Are you all right?" I called.

He grabbed the side of the basket and held tight. "What the hell? I'm okay!"

Angus, who had braced himself against the galley door, stared back at me. "What is going on?"

"A shear," I called back, holding onto the wheel of the *Stargazer* as I guided her path along the fey line. We flew past Grant who ran to the side of his ship. While the fey line was not leading us on the most direct of paths, it was taking us where we needed to go—fast.

"What kind of shear?" Angus yelled back to me. "The wind isn't even blowing!"

"Lily!" Jessup demanded.

"Lily!" Angus echoed.

"It's a fey line! We're riding the ancient path."

"What!" Angus and Jessup yelled in unison.

Angus crawled out of the galley and went to the prow. "I don't see anything. Jessup?" Angus called.

Jessup, who had gotten himself upright again, was gazing out at the horizon. He was silent. "Jessup!" Angus called again.

"Just close your eyes and feel," Jessup yelled back.

He was right, you could feel the crackling sensation of energy all around you. I had felt it before, I just never knew what it was. Not until Arcadia. Reluctantly, Angus did as Jessup suggested. After a few minutes, he turned and went back to the galley. "Let's ride," he said then dropped into the galley.

I stayed the course. Following the fey line, I flew the ship toward London. We flew steady, silent and steady, back home. Robin. It was Robin who had guided us. Thanks to Robin, we could still win the race. The notion both thrilled and frightened me. But I reminded myself that Robin was not Ianthe. This was not a favor that was going to cost me. I trusted Robin.

As we came into London, the glowing light of the line began to weaken. It was like the city had somehow subdued the ancient energy. I pulled off the goggles and safely stowed them in my bag. Once more, we were running on the *Stargazer's* speed alone.

"See anyone?" I asked Jessup as we neared the towers.

"Someone . . . I can't make out who," Jessup called.

London was alive with sound. They'd been waiting for this moment, for the first of the ships to arrive. It was already dusk. The air coming off the Thames was cool. The city was alive with excitement. It was May Day. As we neared the towers, I saw the colorful tents in the streets. They had lit bonfires all along the Thames. As we flew overhead, the crowd cheered.

I eyed the platform. Only one other racing ship was in port. It was the *Gideon*, and the ship was damaged. It must have limped in across country from Edinburgh. We guided the *Stargazer* in like it was just another day. We were just porting at London like we always did. No one even said a word, we just did our job. We'd come home, but we'd come home winners.

Much of the crowd on the platform was cheering. In the streets below, everyone rooted us on. I was proud of the *Stargazer*. She was a symbol of the capabilities of the people of our realm. It moved me to tears to know the people were glad to see us come home first.

Small cannons erupted, shooting streamers of multicolored ribbons into the air. The rainbow of colors twisted in the wind. The excited crowd below cheered. Fireworks dazzled with golden light against the late afternoon sky. I steered the *Stargazer* into dock. Angus threw the anchor lines to the platform crew. We were home. By tapping into the ancient spirit of our realm, we had won. For Byron.

CHAPTER 32

Sour faced, Grant docked the *Comus* about twenty minutes later. And to my great delight, the *Falstaff* came in third. After Bigsby and Grant arrived, the league chairman ushered us all to the winner's platform for what he assured us would be a very special honor. Sal stood waiting on the notables' platform. He waved to me. He was smiling proudly.

"Ladies and gentlemen," the league chairman called, hushing the crowd. "Ladies and gentlemen, let's have a cheer for the *Falstaff, Comus,* and *Stargazer,*" his voice boomed into a megaphone.

From the tower to the streets below, everyone cheered.

"This is a very special day," the league chairman boomed. "Ladies and gentlemen, please welcome a special guest who has come to bestow the awards on the winners."

With a flourish of trumpets, a sea of red velvet bedecked footmen flooded the platform, King George at the center. There was a shocked hush as his majesty, who rarely made public appearances, made his way toward us. Having taken in the magnitude of what they were seeing, the crowd then erupted into a wild cheer. I could not believe it either.

King George took the podium. The league chairman tried to hand him the megaphone, but he brushed the man aside. The monarch needed no assistance. Everyone fell silent.

"Congratulations, winners," King George began. "What a glorious day for racing," he said, motioning to the sky above. "As a boy, Archibald Boatswain must have looked toward the firmament and called down inspiration. How does one travel across heavens? Boatswain used the only tools at his disposal to answer such questions. With these," he said, lifting then turning his hands, "and with this," he added, placing his hand on his heart. "Hands and heart. These are the tools of our airship pilots. It is a profession for the passionate. And before us, we have the most passionate pilots in our realm," he said, winking at me.

"Now, for our third place team," he announced, his voice booming across the sky, "the bronze trophy." The King handed a quivering Bigsby a bronze trophy cast in the shape of an airship.

"For our second place team, the silver trophy," the King said, motioning Grant to come forward and claim his prize. Bowing deeply, his hair falling over his eyes, Grant accepted the award.

"And for our first place winner, the reigning World Champions, and our lovely May Day Queen, we have a special token of our esteem," the King said then motioned two footmen to come forward. With them, they carried a large item hidden under a red velvet drape. Grandstanding a bit, the King removed the cover with a flourish. Under the drape was Boatswain's schematic of the first airship framed elaborately in gold. I motioned for Angus and Jessup to go forward and take the frame.

"Congratulations to the crew of the *Stargazer*," King George cheered. He gestured for me to come forward. He kissed the back of my hand then eyed me curiously. "Woad?" He shook his head. "What a Celt," he added. In one fell swoop, King George delivered a message that everyone could understand: the *Stargazer* was untouchable.

King George waved to the crowd. Everyone cheered loudly. His majesty, again surrounded by a sea of red velvet, made his way to an airship anchored nearby. The king waved once more as the airship pulled up anchor and headed toward Windsor, leaving us all in awe.

CPSIA information can be obtained at www.ICGtesting.com
Printed in the USA
LVOW07s1001180316

479616LV00033B/337/P

ABOUT THE AUTHOR

Melanie Karsak grew up in rural northwestern Pennsylvania where there wasn't much to do but read books and go for hikes. She wrote her first novel, a gripping piece about a 1920s stage actress, when she was 12. Today, Melanie, a steampunk connoisseur, white elephant collector, and caffeine junkie, lives in Florida with her husband and two children. She is an Instructor of English at Eastern Florida State College.

Keep in touch with the author online. She's really nice!

Blog: Melaniekarsak.blogspot.com
Twitter: Twitter.com/MelanieKarsak
Email: melanie@clockpunkpress.com
Facebook: Facebook.com/AuthorMelanieKarsak
Pinterest: Pinterest.com/melaniekarsak/
Authorgraph: Authorgraph.com/authors/MelanieKarsak
Goodreads: Goodreads.com/author/show/6539577.Melanie_Karsak

ANGUS AND JESSUP CONGRATULATED BIGSBY and his crew while I looked for Sal. He emerged from the notables' platform. I waved to him. Grant's sponsors passed by looking more sour than Grant himself.

"My wife," Sal said excitedly, lifting me off the ground and kissing me hard. "A woman with the winds in her heart," he added, setting me back down.

"Wait until she tells you how she managed it," Angus said.

Sal looked curiously at me.

"Later," I said with a grin. Suddenly, I was feeling exhausted.

Sal bent to look at the schematic Jessup was propping up. Duncan joined Angus, hugging his brother tightly. I turned to see Grant, who looked like he'd just been flayed by his sponsors, heading back down the platform toward the *Comus*.

I went after him. "Julius?"

As I had done to him at *The Lancelot Club*, he ignored me.

"Julius?" I called again.

He stopped, his trophy hanging loosely in his hand. "What is it, Lily?"

"I wanted to ask you about your sails. They're legal? The design . . . it's brilliant. Are they detachable? Did you stow them on deck?"

Grant eyed me curiously. "How did you move so fast?" he asked.

"Pardon?"

"Outside Bristol."

I shrugged. "I caught a shear."

"What shear?"

"You didn't feel it?"

Grant pushed his hair behind his ear. His eyes narrowed. "No, I didn't."

"It was just luck. Your sails, however, are bloody brilliant."

"I'm so pleased you admire them," he said sarcastically.

I frowned. "Look, Julius-"

"If you want sails, go to Brittany," he said, interrupting me. "A . . . tinker named Largoët," Grant said then waited for my reaction.

"Largoët?"

Grant smirked. "Congratulations on the win. Good luck in the Prix," he said then hopped onto his ship.

Rattled, I boarded the *Stargazer*. I went astern and looked out at the river. The Thames was usually dark and muddy, but as the sky turned orange and pink, the river reflected the sunset. From the streets below, I heard the voice of the city. It was full of excitement. People were singing the May Day song. Colorful ribbons, snagged by the tree limbs, twisted in the breeze. I caught the scent of roasting meat, peanuts, and baked sweets in the wind. The mix of smells made me feel nauseous. I leaned against the rail. On the Southbank, a stand of hawthorn trees was in full bloom. The sweet scent of their white blossoms forced out the carnival smells. The breeze shook the trees. Petals dusted the water.

Suddenly, light flashed from amongst the trees. Once again, the clockwork fairy fluttered toward me. This time, however, she carried a small package. I held out my hands. The clockwork fairy dropped the item therein then headed back across the river. I opened the package. Inside, I found a necklace. The pendant was a heart carved from simple limestone, but it was sided by clockwork wings. I touched the heart. The wings began to flutter. Digging the fairy goggles from my bag, I pulled them on then looked toward the trees. Under the branches, small winged creatures flitted about in the sparkling, golden light. Robin stood in the center of their glow. He raised his hand. Smiling, I pulled off my hat and goggles then bowed. Robin chuckled, waved once more, then turned and disappeared back into the green.

ACKNOWLEDGEMENTS

A DEBT OF GRATITUDE TO:

My husband and my beloved family for their continued support of my work.

Cat Carlson Amick for her work on and dedication to this series.

Naomi Clewett for her help and encouragement.

Margo Bond Collins for her many contributions to this novel and for teaching me not to use the word snuck.

Toni Lestaz, Mark Fisher, and Michael Hall Jr. for your contributions, big and small, to my writing career.

The Airship Stargazer Ground Crew for helping me spread the word about all things Stargazer! You guys rock!

The bloggers! I owe a massive debt of gratitude to the book bloggers who have embraced my writing and support my works! Thank you so much!